aftertime

a f t e r t i m e

Olaf Georg Klein

Translated from the German by
Margot Bettauer Dembo

NORTHWESTERN UNIVERSITY PRESS
EVANSTON, ILLINOIS

Hydra Books
Northwestern University Press
Evanston, Illinois 60208-4210

Originally published in German under the title *Nachzeit*. Copyright © 1990 by Thomas Müller, Verlag, Berlin. English translation © 1999 by Hydra Books/Northwestern University Press. Published 1999. All rights reserved.

Printed in the United States of America

ISBN 0-8101-1504-2

Library of Congress Cataloging-in-Publication Data

Klein, Olaf Georg, 1955–
  [Nachzeit English]
  Aftertime / Olaf Georg Klein ; translated from the German by Margot Bettauer Dembo.
    p.   cm.
  ISBN 0-8101-1504-2 (cloth)
  I. Dembo, Margot Bettauer. II. Title.
PT2671.L4135N3313   1999
833'.92—dc21   99-19344
                                                                      CIP

The paper used in this publication meets the minimum requirements of the American National Standard for Information Sciences—Permanence of Paper for Printed Library Materials, ANSI Z39.48-1984.

For my sons, Felix and Benjamin,
And for all the world's children

You must dare to be yourself.

—D. H. (Dag Hammarskjöld), *Zeichen der Zeit*

)

I t was not a snap decision. No. It had matured over a long period of time. Granted, for others, even those close to me, this wasn't easy to see. But once I had made up my mind, it was natural, clear, and unavoidable as nothing in my life had ever been. The decision gave me back my freedom. Really, how absurd. What the doctors and nurses are now calling my "return to life" is nothing but a chain of unlucky circumstances.

What a beautiful day it had been. Warm but not hot, with bright dabs of cloud in a spacious sky and a white carpet of petals under the cherry trees. That afternoon, in a shady corner of our lawn, I was lying on a blanket, running my fingertips over its fleecy fabric, and I was watching my father. He sat erect in an armchair, his right leg crossed over the left. His gray hair combed back severely, deep straight lines on his forehead. Now and then, without looking up, he vigorously turned the pages of his book, back and forth; but the rest of the time his eyes moved tirelessly along the printed lines. Noises drifted over from the neighbors' yards: the clatter of dishes, irregular hammering, fragments of music carried by the wind. Father seemed not to hear any of it. I, too, had an open book in front of me, *The Little Prince* by Saint-Exupéry, but I wasn't looking at its pages. I knew much of the text by heart: "There was nothing there but a flash of yellow close to his ankle. He remained motionless for an instant. He did not cry out. He fell as gently as a tree falls. There was not even any sound, because of the sand." It's a good thing I still know these lines by heart. It shows that my memory's in working order.

That afternoon. Again and again I closed my eyes, felt my face, passing my hands along the fine line of nearly straight eyebrows, down to the lightly rounded nostrils, tracing the curvature of my lips, feeling my skin, soft skin covering the cheekbones; or

I spread my fingers and ran them slowly through my hair. Once the sun disappeared behind the gathering clouds, it turned cool.

I see myself again: getting up, folding the blanket, and walking with rapid steps into the house.

My parents had left for the theater. That evening. A few days before they had told me they were planning to go, and they knew I would not go with them.

It was all so matter-of-fact: I asked them whether they had their tickets, and Father reached for his wallet to check; using two fingers I picked a little thread off his jacket; I hugged them and said good-bye, kissed each on the cheek—only fleetingly so as not to give myself away. Then they were off, down a few stairs, and the front door closed. Father went to get the car out of the garage; Mother drove. For weeks, actually for months, ever since I had come back from Kiev, he had not been quite sober. I stood on the porch and watched them drive off. At last I was alone. I felt cold. Shivering, I rubbed my hands together, pulled on a sweater, and went into my father's study.

Did all this happen just a few days ago? Barely a week ago? No. That can't be. It must have been years ago.

I stood in front of the bookshelves, passed my right hand over the spines of the books, absentmindedly spelling out the titles: *The Principle of Dialogue, The Origins of History, History of German Literature* . . . ; then I took a few steps, stopped, and randomly took down one of the books. Was I prompted by some memory? Attracted by the color of the book's cover? Should I open it? This one or that one? Perhaps it contains one last essential bit of information for me? But how was I to find it?

I can still feel the book in my hand, can still feel its weight, can see myself leafing irresolutely through its pages, careful not to dislodge the small scraps of paper inserted here and there by my father. Perhaps there's a clue here? No. Not here. But then my father had a large library.

I say "had"; but he *has* it still. Only it's all so long ago; it's long since been: past perfect. I sat down in the chair at his desk near the window, glanced out into the garden, looked at the framed photos standing on his desk: a man gazing into the distance, his eyes wide open, seemingly observing something that interests him, unwilling to stop looking at it, something that remains concealed from me. A woman stands next to him and looks at me with dark, almost black eyes. Her left eyebrow a little higher than the right, her mouth slightly open, lending her face a look of childish wonderment; no doubt she put on that delicate necklace especially for this photograph. In front of the bedroom mirror. Perhaps. And in a third picture, a dreamy young girl, naive, with straight, long hair of which she is obviously proud, a yearning mouth, a delicately curved nose, and freckles she surely detests.

Slowly I put the photos back where they had stood, as carefully as if I were a guest in someone else's house.

❙

How quietly he always closes the window when he arrives. How cautiously he walks, how careful his movements. As though he doesn't want to frighten me. Each time, this long pause before my lips are willing to formulate words and sentences that seem like messages from another time.

❙

I see myself going into the living room and gently stroking the tablecloth there. Never before have I felt the material so intensely, never before has there been such a tacit understanding between me and these inanimate things. They did not betray me. They remained silent.

In prior weeks I had often entered this room, my hands clasped tightly together, in my head the prickling sensation of thousands of crawling ants, under my skin a tension that didn't know how and where to find release. How often I just wanted to go on a rampage; to yank the tablecloth and vase off the table; to rip the pictures off the walls; to smash that revolting ballet dancer because she didn't want to stop twirling no matter what was happening around her; to punch holes through the fall landscape with the wind-ravaged trees and the unreachable distant horizon; to upend the table and the chairs; throw the radio and the TV through the window, shattering the glass; and to slit open the upholstered chairs and sofa. Yes, I had wanted to punish these things because they were deluding me into believing that everything had remained the same, that the quiet, eerie destruction had not yet reached this house. Now, finally, I had wanted them to reflect what had happened to me.

And that evening: stillness, intimacy, undreamed-of peace. The gentle touch of fingertips on fabric. The handle felt cool in my hand as I gently pulled the door closed. I had stepped through this door innumerable times as a child, as a girl, as a woman, angry, laughing, hesitant, and never paid attention to it, its structure, the irregularities in the wood, the cool brass handle with its slight curvature that seemed made to fit my hand.

There were other books lying on Father's night table. I picked up the one on top of the pile. What would be the first sentence he would read the next time he lay in bed, unable to fall asleep? I opened it at random and read: "As always she was warm and friendly. There was no trace of agitation or concern."

I still remember those words. That's reassuring. A good sign. Back then. Back then? Only a few days ago these words frightened me. They seemed so strangely appropriate, as though someone knowing my situation had written those sentences. I stared at the paper until the letters swam back and forth, the words snaked up and down, and everything finally disappeared behind a veil. I see myself replacing the book and pressing the balls of my thumbs over my eyelids to dispel the fog. I see myself as if I had always been able to observe myself from the outside through the eyes of a stranger.

Turning around hesitantly, like a blind woman, I took a few careful steps. Then I opened my eyes and glanced sideways into the mirror. Above the wooden footboard of my parents' beds there appear two, four, six hands. They are wrapped in sleepwear but are still identifiable because of the difference in their sizes, and they begin a half-serious, half-grotesque game: They correct and scold each other; they ask things of one another and make mistakes; they are clumsy and cunning; they constantly change their clothes. I see them play all the childhood games my parents played with me in their bedroom, Sunday morning after Sunday morning. Once again they pass before my eyes at a mad pace, faster and faster, until I tear myself away and place myself resolutely between the apparitions and the mirror.

At first the woman in the mirror stands absolutely still. Then, step by step, slowly and inexorably, she comes closer. She lifts her hands and simultaneously attacks me and wards me off.

Finally her hands are restrained by two other hands; fingertips touch fingertips, pressing against each other with equal pressure; but her head and her staring, scary eyes come ever closer.

I

The glass of the mirror was cold on my forehead. I took a step back, passed my hands over my face, my neck, feeling my small firm breasts through my sweater. No one will ever kiss them again, I thought; no one will caress them. With a self-mocking smile I shook my head.

What absurd emotions. To stand before a mirror and become sentimental, after the decision I had made. How stupid. Quick as a flash I spun around on my right foot. To be a dancer. Mad. Possessed. Turning, always turning. I left the room without another look. I stopped briefly outside the music room, but the closed door rebuffed me. Slowly now, one foot in front of the other. I pressed down on the handle of the front door. The door was locked. Then, without making a sound, I went up the wooden staircase to my room, avoiding all the places where the boards would creak. There was no one in the house. It didn't matter. It was only a game. I wanted to prove to myself: I am absolutely sure. I can trust myself. My plan will succeed, just as I am climbing the stairs at this very moment without making the slightest sound.

Then: switch off the hall light, walk into my room, carefully close the door without turning on the light.

In the preceding days and weeks I had unobtrusively put my room in order, had torn up letters, including those from Laura and those from Ralph; had torn up my files, my school notes, my diaries. For hours I sat in front of the stove and watched as these papers instantly curled up in the flames as though in rebellion, in a silent protest before they were engulfed, became charred, and finally disintegrated into white ash. And now I stood there, in my room. Happy that everything had been put in order. At peace. For a long time I had been working toward this moment without admitting it to myself.

All my movements were sure, aware, and precise, as though I had rehearsed them throughout my life for just this evening. I watched myself as one watches a show, a one-woman performance. Put a record on the phonograph, wipe the dust off the record with a cloth, drape the mirror the way one does in a house where someone has just died, a house of mourning—the end of vanity in the face of death. No, vanity doesn't end. I looked at the pendulum of the grandfather clock and wondered whether I should stop it from swinging back and forth. I didn't. For some time I stood at the window, thinking: The world will go on. The trees will keep growing and bring forth leaves and blossoms, will bear fruit, will wither, and so on, all the unfathomable years that will lose themselves in the gray mist of an unformed future.

I resolutely drew the curtains, lay down on the bed, and closed my eyes. The incision was unexpectedly gentle, the piano music coming from the record player became softer, ever softer, and then it stopped.

I

Why does he even bother to come to the hospital? Why does he visit me? Given his religious convictions, he can't possibly condone what I did. Let him go see the other women here, but not me. Why doesn't he leave me alone? Having once and for all decided to choose silence, why am I not silent? I want to be silent again. The next time I'll endure that interminable pause and remain silent.

It's really absurd to be here again. Here. Conscious. I was done with life, had left everything behind me. Finally. Irrevocably. Nonetheless they brought me back.

I come to. Not knowing anything, neither inside nor outside; not knowing where I am and what's happening; I hear buzzing, ticking sounds, an indistinct whispering; I see white, red, blue dots, a glaring light, hazy figures. Where nothing was supposed to be, there's suddenly something. And—incredulous at first, not trusting my senses—as I begin to differentiate things, colors, sounds, to relate them to one another, to penetrate the chaos, the impossible gradually becomes clear: I'm back again after having taken leave forever. Surrounded by ministering aides, shackled to a bed, tubes and needles in me—a lump of flesh robbed of its own will. Intensive care unit as torture chamber. Doctors as inquisitors. They demand a confession from me. As if I hadn't been confessing all along. Confessions, spoken and unspoken. They demand that I agree with the universally obligatory dogma: You must live! No. I don't have to. I don't want to. Not any longer. Not like this. I have the right to decide what to do with my own life.

"You will be grateful to us one day." Words. Nothing but words. No, I won't be grateful. Never. I spat at the first face that emerged from the fog and came toward me smiling—a mocking, grimacing face. To spit. It was the only thing I could do to express my contempt, my resistance. To reasonable eyes, an outrage.

So what! I don't want to have anything to do with that kind of reasoning. I don't understand it. I don't want to understand it. Tens of thousands of people are exposed to infertility, lingering sickness, and death from cancer. It is accepted as a "side effect," as an "accident," and then they fire up the reactor again and continue with the fission, calmly and indifferently, wrapped in the delusion of the theory of probability. This is "reasonable."

Yet when I, who was struck by these "side effects," decide what to do with my damaged life, I am treated as if I were not quite sane. To them, this is "reasonable," too.

Why do they find my decision so unbearable? Why do they go to such lengths to dissuade me from taking the path I have chosen? Why no comparable efforts to eliminate the causes of so many unintended deaths? I don't understand this reasoning.

I can't blame my parents for trying to bring me back. It's a sort of reflex: protecting your own offspring. Except they don't understand that they are powerless, that they can no longer protect and preserve.

I should excuse their blindness. But, damn it, they have to leave me alone now, have to stop hiding from the truth. After all, they know what happened to their daughter. Yet they refuse to accept it and continue to wage a futile battle. One always fights most desperately for that which is already a lost cause: a past love, a destroyed landscape, a fading life. Some mechanism, some predisposition, keeps us from recognizing the point in time when it is still possible to turn back, when salvation is still possible.

My parents will want to visit me. I no longer want that. I can't bear it. How can I look them in the eye? See their sorrow, their despair, the morbid optimism with which they try to deceive themselves? And why should they have to see me lying here? In their view, I was saved. Yet lost. It would all become even more unbearable, for me and also for them. No, I have said good-bye to them for good.

True, less than a year ago when I came home after studying abroad, I played along; I also suppressed the truth. I wanted to be normal then, just like everybody else. A human being among other human beings, a woman among other women. Back then, I found it annoying to be asked, on some pretext or other, to come to well-intentioned support groups, to hear reassurances or words that brought false comfort, or subtle threats made behind padded doors. I didn't want to be spied on when I received a phone call at work, I didn't want to be seen as someone who carried something sinister, something monstrous, within her. I didn't want to be pitied or treated with this special consideration that in effect ostracized me. I didn't want eyes averted and conversations breaking off whenever I approached. I just wanted to go on leading a simple, ordinary, even superficial life, to do the things that gave me pleasure, and to continue to ignore my own condition. I wanted to forget what the doctor in Kiev had said, to blot out that part of my past, to banish it from my life story. Yet, other people's behavior and the looks they gave me kept forcing me to return to the time I wanted to repress. And now? Now that I understand my situation and have accepted it, now that I have made my decision, they want to do everything in their power to deter me from the course I have chosen.

I

Why did it have to happen to me? Why in that particular place? Why at a time when I was so close to it? No. I don't want to persist with these senseless questions. I don't want to rethink again and again what can't be changed.

These mental images. Always these images of me on the boat that spring night, happy, unsuspecting, looking forward to going home, dancing, unconcernedly breathing in the spring air in which something was suspended that I inhaled but did not exhale. Something that accumulated in my body, moving on mysteriously only to become concentrated somewhere within me, there to gain in strength. And of all this, I knew—nothing. Why didn't the calamity occur three months later? After I had already left? Or at some other place in the world?

Oh, stop! Don't keep asking yourself these idiotic questions. They're unanswerable. And they can't help you. They're horrible. But what else can I do? Should I compare myself to others? Think about my situation in relative terms? "Just look at him or her; compared with them you're well off!" No. I don't want to console myself with the knowledge that others are worse off than I am. Even if there are a thousand, ten thousand, or a hundred thousand of them.

I wanted to go on living like those who were never there. Carefree. Unconcerned. Nonchalant. To go on with my life as though nothing had happened.

No. Not now. Now I don't want that anymore. I've had enough. I've made up my mind. I have no desire for this futile rebellion against fate. A fate inflicted on me by others.

There will be nothing left once I've shed my sick shell. Perhaps a few memories that some people still have of me, dusty documents, useless report cards. No metamorphosis is to be expected.

I'm not a caterpillar that will turn into a butterfly. As a child I used to sit in our garden day after day observing iridescent caterpillars, eating, wriggling their way through the grass. I refused to go inside when it rained; I refused to go in for supper. Because I didn't want to miss the wonderful moment of transformation. Who was it who told me the unbelievable: that a little creeping worm would turn into a soaring colorful butterfly? Why did I never get to see this marvelous transformation?

I will never sprout wings.

My God, I've heard about the firemen who were the first to arrive at the scene of the disaster, without protective clothing, so close to that radioactive monster. They got stuck in the boiling tar. I heard about the doctors who, right after the catastrophe, waded through the vomit in cloth shoes, through the stinking, radioactive white death that covered the floors of the hospital halls and sickrooms. I know that those same doctors are now themselves lying in hospital beds with unstoppable hemorrhages, without hair—emaciated skeletons, full of hope before each operation or transplant, yet knowing deep down that none of this will help them, that they are merely being subjected to desperate experiments. I know how many volunteered. They had no inkling what effects the radiation would have on their health, their lives. Or could it be that they did know? And what if they did? Did they have a choice?

And I, at that time, I was—merely—aboard a boat, dancing, and the next day I went swimming and took a sunbath. And yet, I'm now lying here.

▌

Why can't I keep quiet? Why do I yell at him when he comes to see me, and why do I cry when I'm alone? At night when everyone is asleep, why do I scream into the darkness: "I have a right to my life. Damn it, listen to me." Nobody hears me. Nothing changes. Nothing helps.

I've made my decision, and I won't go back on it. It's all absurd. And it will remain pointless. Stop thinking about it. Go to sleep now. At long last, go to sleep.

I

There was no need for me to go away to school. No need to go to Kiev, that fateful city. To leave the place of my childhood, our house on the outskirts of Berlin where I grew up, an only child. After all, there was a university in the city. I could have stayed and studied there.

I needn't have left you, Father; you who always appeared to me so tall, so imposing. You would raise your bushy dark eyebrows whenever you were surprised. They would form a solid black line above your eyes when you found fault with me. Your movements were measured and calm, never hectic. At home you said little about the university and the lectures and seminars you gave there. But you took me seriously. I was content to have you as my father and would have had no reason to leave.

Or to leave you either, Mother. For me you always remained the beautiful woman you once were—with long black hair that you liked to wear loose when you came home in the afternoon to be with me after six hours in your laboratory at the hospital.

I still see you lifting the cover of the piano with your slender white fingers, setting up the music; you throw your head back, shaking it slightly to make your hair fall backward over your shoulders. I remember the energy and ease of your playing: how your fingers lightly touched the keys, how your whole body responded to the music. Again I hear the music spreading through the room, floating like a filmy, finely woven cloth on which one can nevertheless lie and dream. Sitting there at the piano you looked like an angel carrying a mysterious message that held the secret for happiness. I could never understand why angels in pictures are usually blond. For me angels have black hair.

I can still see us making music together. You are playing the piano; I, the flute. And I thought: If I play well with an angel, I myself will get to be a little like an angel. That was then. Childish muddled thoughts. I wanted Father to like me. After our little concert I wanted him to carry me on his shoulders through our overgrown garden. I wanted him to toss me up in the air, to catch me, and to follow my exuberant childish commands without protest.

I was happy at home and couldn't understand my classmates when they complained about their parents. I still remember clearly how, from time to time, we would sit down together for our little "family conferences." We were each allowed to say what we didn't like, what bothered us about the family. I could speak my mind and you listened. Problems were discussed without recriminations. Feelings were taken seriously and not ridiculed, even if at first they were incomprehensible to the other members of the family. In that way no anger or grudges accumulated, and we almost always found a way to arrive at a genuine compromise.

These family conferences failed in only one decisive area— your foolish jealousy, Father, going back to the time I had my first little boyfriend. You made compulsive attempts not to let it show, even though it was obviously unpleasant for you. Still. Whenever a boy came to see me, you paced restlessly through the house, dropping dishes, knocking over flower vases, spilling your coffee, burning yourself at the stove. I could always expect some minor mishap, and only after the boy had left were you able to pull yourself together again. Mother laughed, but it got on my nerves. And that's why, one evening at supper, you asked me how I would feel about going to a university in another city. To me this was quite unimportant, but I still recall every detail about that evening. I was going to go dancing with a young man. And you started in on this business: about distancing oneself, becoming mature, finding one's own way, and so forth. While I was away at college, you said, you would finish the attic, put in a separate kitchen, install a shower—what plans you had! I just kept looking at the clock.

I didn't want to be late for my date because of such ridiculous trivia, and I can still hear myself, bored and groaning, saying:

"Okay. Okay." I can hear the exact tone of my voice, with its subliminal: Why don't you leave me alone. How relieved I was when, at last, I was able to leave. I jumped up, slammed the door behind me, grabbed my jacket, and ran off.

|

That evening no one knew that this conversation would lead to a calamity. I don't remember if, later on, we spoke again about the university where I was to study. But your words that evening continued to have an effect on my thinking. Subliminally. Like a judgment. In a macabre sense it became exactly that: a prejudgment. A prejudgment.

One day, during my third year in high school, I decided on the spur of the moment to apply for admission to the university in Leipzig. Just like that. A gut reaction. It wasn't your decision, Father. It was mine. No matter how oddly it came into being. And this decision had nothing to do with Kiev, nothing to do with the calamity.

The offer from Kiev came much later, through my high school: I could apply to study abroad in my major; there were still openings; my schoolwork was more than adequate; and the school would recommend me.

True, that first decision to go to another city made the next decision inevitable, prepared the way. Nevertheless, it was I who decided. I was curious about the USSR. You are not to blame. Damn it, you are not to blame. Not even indirectly. Once and for all, stop reproaching yourself! Stop interpreting my behavior as though it were directed against you! That's not at all how it happened.

|

At first it was just nonchalance on my part, a lack of serious reflection. I had no idea what consequences my decision would have. Anxiety about the distance between us and the length of time I would be away came later. To be 750 miles from home for many years with just brief interruptions, cut off from my familiar environment, far from my beloved home. No chance for a quick visit to see you on weekends. Away from the landscape I was used to, away from the Mark Brandenburg heath, the gnarled, knobby pines, the serene lakes, and walks along sandy paths in the evenings. But this anxiety didn't surface until shortly before my final examination, by which time I had already been accepted at the university and my departure from home was getting closer. Only then did many things I had taken for granted become precious to me. For the first time I felt sad, with a vague sense that I would be leaving behind something I would not find again when I came back years later. Although I could have had no inkling of the insurmountable divide that would subsequently rise between the "before" and the "after."

|

Father, I know you felt guilty after my return because it was you who had originally suggested I might go to a university in another city in the GDR, and you who then advised me to accept the offer to study abroad. I know that at the time you had a problem and you thought it would be solved if I left home. But I also know how hard it was for you to let me go. I sensed your inner conflict. It wasn't your fault that this accident, this catastrophe, occurred near the place where I was studying. Not at all. Do you hear me? Once and for all, forget this damned notion of yours that if you hadn't made the suggestion, none of this would have happened. But I can't talk you out of it anymore. And you yourself can't either.

|

We can't escape the effects of the forces we set in motion. After my return the silence at home reached into all our lives, even though we didn't want it to do so. Our conversations became ever shorter, the sentences briefer, the pauses between them longer and longer. Each word was weighed before it was spoken.

At first the silence covered only the last months of my time at the university. But it grew and grew and encompassed ever wider areas of our everyday lives.

Is that the way I wanted it? Yes and no. I didn't want to be reminded of the accident and the time that followed. So, on the one hand, I found the silence agreeable. It meant that at home, at least, nothing would be churned up, I wouldn't have to grapple with these nagging, agonizing memories. On the other hand, I felt a quiet longing for the candor and mutual trust that used to exist between us. It was absurd. Whenever you steered the conversation around to those critical months, I changed the subject. But once you finally accepted the situation and no longer mentioned it, I silently reproached you for it. Either way, it didn't suit me. The catastrophe stood between us, impenetrable and insurmountable. But, Father, I never held you responsible for my going abroad to study. Never. Please understand that!

It was an entirely different encounter, a different circumstance, that led to my decision. There was one man who could have kept me from going to Kiev, even after everything had already been decided. There was one brief moment—still important to me, even now—when I hesitated. More important than all the other discussions, arrangements, or decisions. Everything would have changed had I given in then to this feeling, this fleeting notion.

❙

Pictures. Pictures. I constantly see pictures before me. I can't lie here anymore. I have to go to sleep now. It's so hot in this room. I ought to drink something. Or perhaps I should open the window. Or call the nurse. Or . . . Oh . . .

❙

The prom. I can still see the parents, the teachers, and us, the new graduates. At first, kidding around, and then trying to put on solemn faces while sneaking sidelong glances at the cold buffet. Diplomas are handed out and carefully tucked away by our parents to protect them from spilled drinks and grease spots. Champagne bottles are uncorked, speeches are made: Now life begins in earnest . . . graduation is only the beginning . . . you have reached the top of the first hill; the mountain range still lies ahead of you.

But I felt as though I were already on the mountaintop. Fathers waltzed with their daughters, sons with their mothers — stiff, awkward, and embarrassed. Whatever happened to my light blue dress?

Doesn't matter. It really doesn't matter at all now. But it was lovely. Cut low in front and back; I actually could feel the material on my skin. That was the first time I had put my hair up. How the fathers of the other students looked at me! I drew their stares like a magnet, was aware of them, and wasn't shy. Father, you were so proud of your daughter, of her report card; she long ago forgot the kind words you said to her. But I'll never forget how you looked: happy and wistful at the same time, seemingly unable to decide between the two feelings. Mother surreptitiously stroked my hair. The band played waltzes, oldies, and new wave music, all jumbled together. And I danced with Ralph.

|

Strange, I can still vividly recall what I felt for Ralph that evening and during those weeks, as though everything that came later never happened.

You were so quiet, almost shy. For years you were in my class and I didn't even notice you. Then, when I did, I thought you were rather boring. You never participated in any of our practical jokes; you showed the same friendliness to everyone. Yet, you were good-looking: black hair, shy blue eyes, and rather narrow lips. Not until we were studying for the examinations did we get to know each other better.

I got accustomed to your calm, considerate ways. Suddenly what had once bothered me about you, I now liked. I was glad that you weren't moody, that you kept every date. I also liked the quiet, contemplative way you looked at me. It's just that even then you weren't the least bit impulsive. Although that bothered me, I found myself more and more frequently glancing at your slender hands, the even rounded shape of your fingernails, wondering secretly whether you could be tender.

I

At the prom, I danced only with you. As long as Father was there I felt I was constantly being watched. I sensed what he was going through, and I didn't want him to knock over drinks "inadvertently" or miss the glass when he poured champagne. But then I brought you to our table. Just like that. Father clinked glasses with us. He was calm, chatted cordially with you, but not once did he make eye contact. Later, I saw Mother taking Father's hand and talking earnestly with him. When I came back to our table, she spoke in a deliberately loud voice, "Our daughter is old enough. Let's go now. She'll be able to find her way home." What a surprised look Father gave me, as though he were seeing me from afar, as though he were consciously aware of me for the first time. He nodded absentmindedly, hugged me. And then he stood there, undecided. Mother, quite firm, turned and walked toward the door. Hesitantly Father followed her, but not without stopping and ceremoniously saying good-bye to people at various tables. At the door he looked around once more, searching for me among the dancers. And as he stood there, so forlorn, he seemed suddenly older, less tall than usual. I waved to him again; he smiled, closed his eyes for a moment, and then followed Mother outside. Of course you weren't aware of any of that. Why should you have been? But after that I danced and danced with you, and I was so very happy.

How long ago that was. How unbelievably long ago. After a while the lights in the hall began to hurt our eyes; we drained the champagne in our glasses; chairs were being piled up on the tables. It was over. We held hands and walked through the streets; we kissed and then we were at your house, in your room. I wonder if you remembered this later on. It was so quiet. I kept looking at the posters you had tacked and taped on the walls and on the large dark brown armoire. Even though I knew them well. After all, I had seen them while we were studying for the exams.

Those long-haired, sweaty musicians bent over their guitars. But what else was I supposed to look at. I sat on your bed, but you sat on the chair. And we smoked cigarettes. Because we were embarrassed. Whenever your hand reached toward the ashtray to flick the ash off your cigarette, I also just happened to be flicking the ash off mine and, as if by accident, I touched your hand. I noticed how you looked at me from time to time. But when I tried to look into your eyes, you turned away. So I went back to staring at the posters of the musicians. This went on for a long time. Fortunately, I finally took your hand. And still you made believe you didn't notice. You were so reticent. And I was so receptive. But it was a good thing you were like that, exactly like that. Later, I was embarrassed because of the sheet. "Never mind," you dismissed it, "Don't worry about it," and "You could have told me."

What should I have told you? Afterward we lay together, my head on your arm, your warm hand on my stomach. I can still hear your calm regular breathing. The birds awoke, it began to get light outside. Were you really sleeping? I lay there awake the entire time; I had imagined it would be quite different. So much more wonderful. I intended to get up quietly and get dressed. Just then you opened your eyes and asked me, "Are you leaving already?"

"Go back to sleep," I said. But you insisted on walking me part of the way home.

I

It was lovely that morning, walking side by side, holding hands. Until I began to cry. I was ashamed of my tears. I leaned my head against your shoulder, and you asked, "Are you sorry?" But I wasn't sorry at all. There was no way you could understand. I couldn't explain it to you then, this vague feeling. I wanted to be near you. I wanted to stay home, not to go away, not to study in that faraway foreign city. Anything, anything, just not to be so far away. At that instant I had this strong feeling, this clear thought: I would simply stay here. And what did I do? I cried and leaned against your shoulder. But I didn't have the strength to assert myself against common sense, against all the arrangements and plans that had been made, including admission to the university. If only I had followed my instincts! At that point I could still have turned back! Then everything would have turned out differently. It would have been so simple:

. . . I AM SORRY TO DISAPPOINT THE CONFIDENCE YOU HAVE PLACED IN ME, BUT UNFORTUNATELY IT IS IMPOSSIBLE . . . FOR PERSONAL REASONS . . . BECAUSE I AM PREGNANT . . . UNFORTU- NATELY I CANNOT ACCEPT THE OPPORTUNITY YOU HAVE OFFERED ME . . . DEAR FATHER, PLEASE UNDERSTAND THAT UNDER THESE CIRCUMSTANCES . . . IT SIMPLY IS NOT POSSIBLE . . . I WANT TO LIVE WITH THIS MAN . . . I WANT TO HAVE HIS CHILD . . .

But I didn't do it. After all, I wasn't pregnant and I didn't want to be a sentimental fool. So I wiped away my tears and said tersely, "No, no, I'm not sorry. Really, it's all right."

I had made my decision. A bad decision. At that cursed moment I had set my life on a definitive course. Against my instinct. Against my inner voice. And we walked on as though nothing had happened. And the woods was still the same and the road was the same, but they could all have been different. Then I would never have gone off to that place; then I wouldn't be lying here.

We made a date to see each other again a couple of days later and said good-bye halfway between your place and mine. I can still feel your soft lips on mine, see myself walking away in my blue dress; I wasn't even cold. After a few steps, I turned around and waved to you; then I walked on and on, and on, thinking, Now he's going home to his musicians, into his room, into our bed.

I

It was already daylight when I got home. Not the least bit tired, I set the breakfast table, made coffee. Father was surprised to see me up so early and tried to tease me about it. Mother told him to leave me alone.

I was a woman. And was that all there is to it? I had waited for this, had been afraid of it. Was this what everybody made such a fuss about? Everything was still the same: my movements in preparing breakfast, the colors, the sounds. Except now there was one less mystery, I wasn't tired in the morning, and my room seemed so small.

The vacation began. We went swimming or to get ice cream or to the movies. We were affectionate to each other. But it wasn't the sort of love that overcomes all obstacles, that breaks down barriers. It was a love that conformed to the demands of the world, to what seemed essential and what actually was essential.

There was no longer any question: It was to be five years at the university in Kiev for me. And three years in the army for you, after which you'd get your degree in physics. Separation. Yes. But we would write and never forget each other. Of course the intervals between our letters would not get longer; we would not stop writing to each other altogether one day. That is what we promised each other, what we hoped, and yet did not really believe.

It happened as it was bound to happen. The years passed. The only surprise was that shortly before the end of my time at the university, another letter from you arrived. Perhaps I should have thrown it away, unread. But I was pleased. It came at just the right time, shortly before my return. After five years, so far from home. Two days before the catastrophe of which no one had an inkling.

|

During the time we spent together after the prom there was no way we could have known about any of this. We didn't think much about the future. It was so uncertain, so vast and undecided. Everything was quite unreal. And then saying good-bye did hurt. In those days.

There were all sorts of formalities to take care of before the end of the vacation; I had to pack things and send them ahead, had to say good-bye to relatives and friends. I did all this with amazing detachment. As though I weren't directly involved, like an extra in a stage play directed and acted by others. I watched what was happening to me and going on around me, almost amused, yet always wondering. Not until I was actually at the airport with my parents, surrounded by our old suitcases that reminded me of former vacation trips, did I feel that all this was really happening to me. While I waited for my flight to be announced, I saw others who would later be at the university with me. Now they were standing there just as lost as I was, surrounded by parents and friends.

I can still hear the clatter of the airport signboard listing departures; a last embrace; then a woman in a uniform casually looks over my flight ticket. I hurry through the narrow passageway, turn around once, and see that you, Father, and Mother are holding hands, and then I disappear behind the metal-framed frosted-glass door. After taking a few steps up the gangway to the airplane I wave once more toward the observation platform, even though I can no longer make you out.

The plane stood on the tarmac for a long time before it finally began to move. Then it rolled faster and faster down the runway; we were pressed back into our seats. For a second I thought the earth would not release us; the plane would be smashed to smithereens in the nearby forest . . .

We flew above clouds that only in the beginning permitted a brief glimpse of the earth below. I felt cut off from everything, belonging nowhere, set adrift, helpless as the plane raced toward a city of which I knew only the name, had seen only a few pictures. I would have liked to turn back and land at home again or at least remain in this suspended condition between heaven and earth, between departure and arrival, between my own and the new foreign language. But the plane arrived, landing in Kiev. Strange-looking vehicles drove up and drove off again; officials in Russian uniforms inspected our passports and baggage. I smelled strange smells I could not identify. Life in another language had begun.

How I cried the first few nights. Only the hectic activity, the formalities, the endless visits to the offices of the authorities, and the unfamiliar impressions blotted out my homesickness for a few hours at a time. I wrote to my parents and to Ralph every day and begged them to write back soon. But it was an eternity before their first letters reached me.

At some point—I don't know exactly when—I no longer knew

where I belonged, where I should drop my inner anchor. In the place I had come from and hoped one day to return to, but to which at the moment I felt less and less connected, except for a boundless longing that sometimes overcame me? Or in Kiev, where I now lived and where my friends were, where I spoke a new language? But at some time or other, willing or not, I had arrived. Inwardly. I felt myself sending down roots, I sensed the city gradually becoming my home. My past, my childhood, seemed like a distant, unreal dream. Somehow, in another language, one becomes a different person, dreams different dreams, feels different; one *is* different. Going home after these five years would have been difficult for me in any case. But under these circumstances . . .

I

My last winter in Kiev was cold, the thermometer often hit twenty-two degrees below zero. Enormous quantities of snow covered the streets, piling up along the curbs. Again and again, as the snow became gray and unsightly, it was covered by a new white film. I still see myself waiting for a bus, watching the soundless campaign waged by the falling white flakes against the brown-black slush spatters lining the edge of the street; still see myself sitting across from some old women on a cold suburban train, women wearing woolen kerchiefs and smelling of garlic who, despite the frosted windows, knew exactly where they had to get off. I see myself lighting a candle because the electricity in the dorm would often fail for minutes or hours at a time. Not a single conversation took place during that long winter that didn't anticipate the coming spring. I longed for the sun, warm weather; I wanted to take long walks again, go swimming, unpack my T-shirts and summer dresses.

But spring simply refused to come. It was as though nature were holding her breath, as though she wanted to disrupt the seasonal cycle so that later she could capriciously let winter pass right into summer.

Then suddenly there were tomatoes and cucumbers in the market, summer dresses were fluttering on all the balconies, and the trees that had been bare so long turned green overnight, called back to life along the streets and in the squares.

During this first week of early summer I would sit on a wooden park bench for hours watching, day by day, as the leaves unfolded and young couples strolled the tree-lined avenues arm in arm or holding each other around the waist. Everything and everyone were stretching and opening up, trying to shake off the overlong winter, to enjoy the late spring they had already thought lost. At last the air was no longer an icy enemy but rather a pleasantly warm wrap. I listened avidly to the weather report for this last weekend in April. The sun would shine, they said, it would be hot, and I made plans.

I would go swimming or at least I'd go to the beach, and in the evening perhaps I would go dancing. And why not? It was all so simple, so beautiful, so incredibly beautiful.

ǀ

Toward evening Laura burst into the room we shared. She was quite out of breath and was already in the middle of the room by the time the door loudly slammed shut. She looked around with those sharp, lively eyes of hers that never focused for long on any one thing. Then she came toward me, slowly, deliberately, and suddenly brought her hand down on the book I was reading.

"You'll never guess what I have here! Tickets for a boat cruise with dancing, and you're going, too. No argument."

I tried to tell her, "I was planning to go dancing, too. Really. I decided to, just this afternoon."

"Oh, you're lying," Laura said, and I can still hear the mischievous tone in her voice. "You would have buried your nose in your books again. Admit it. Oh well, it doesn't matter. In any case you're coming along, and that's nice."

That's how she talked, how she was. Good-natured and frenetic. Laura. Fortune's freckled favorite. I wonder how you are now. Not that I'm worried about you. You always came through. You always did the right thing, instinctively. You're probably doing fine.

For how long had we been rooming together? Two years, or was it already three? Gradually we had become friends. Surprising really since we were so different in almost every way. You took life so lightly, were always in a good mood, were invariably lucky: At examination time you were assigned the very topic you had by chance picked to study; you turned up at the theater or at the concert hall box office just as someone was returning his tickets; in every waiting line you just happened to know someone standing at the head of the line. You had a guardian angel, a seventh sense, or you were simply born lucky. I often envied you.

I still remember how unhappy I was once when I burned the food I was cooking for our dinner. All that effort, wasted. I sat down and cried. A few months later the same thing happened to you. And what did you do? You were glad.

"Come on, let's go out to eat," you said. "Now we've got an excuse." And in the restaurant you met a former friend and re-kindled your relationship. Your conclusion: "If I hadn't burned dinner, I wouldn't have met him again."

Your philosophy worked. For you. I still see the mischievous smile that played around your mouth, spreading all the way up to your eyes in tiny creases. In the beginning it made me feel insecure, confused. After a while I got used to it and no longer felt you were laughing at me. During our vacation when I went with you to visit your parents in the small town where you grew up, I saw the same smile on your father's face.

Because I took many things so seriously, they became serious. Much of the schoolwork was slow going. I was often depressed and sad for reasons not clear to me. Nowadays I wonder how you were able to put up with me.

But that day it all seemed to come together beautifully. My wish and your wish and my joy and your joy. Everything.

I had often been to that large lake north of the city. Everyone called it the "Sea." Fishing with friends, sailing with fellow students, swimming, or walking along the shore. I had watched the passenger boats and the hydrofoils as they majestically, elegantly moved away from the shore, little sailboats swarming around them. For quite some time I had longed to go on one of these boats and had repeatedly postponed it, or there were no tickets left, or something else had prevented it.

This was my last summer in Kiev. My last chance to go on a cruise, and with Laura, no less.

That evening we boarded the boat in high spirits. I still remember how it cast off, how quietly and powerfully it sailed out of the little harbor. The water swirled at the stern, and we left behind waves crowned with foamy whitecaps. Slowly the shoreline disappeared.

A band played, and, whenever the musicians rested, a frenzied disc jockey put Stones records on the turntable. Laura knew several other people onboard, went over to them, laughed and talked with them, gesticulating, now and then looking toward me. I didn't feel like meeting anyone. I wanted to dance, but otherwise I wanted to be by myself.

Whenever I felt too hot, I went up on deck. How mild a night it was. This particular night. Dressed only in a white T-shirt and jeans, no sweater or jacket, I faced into the headwind and didn't feel cold. Taking deep breaths of the mild air, I spread my arms to feel the force of the wind more intensely. Full of joy, I wanted to rise up and fly, just as, when I was a child, I had wanted to be a bird with broad wings and beautiful feathers so that I could soar effortlessly through the air. Up there you could romp exuberantly without bumping into things, without scraping your knees, without falling; you could reach faraway destinations without getting painful blisters on your feet. That evening, during that infinite night, I was once again—as I hadn't been in a long time—close to taking off, to flying.

The shore lights disappeared in the distance; elsewhere other lights appeared unexpectedly. The ship's engine worked quietly and methodically, making the floorboards vibrate slightly. It wasn't until I had gone up on deck for the third or fourth time that I felt a strange irritation in my throat. If you're this happy you won't get sick, I thought. If you're happy. I'm not going to catch a cold in this weather. Strange. What was that indefinable metallic taste in my mouth that would not go away?

I went down to get something to drink and returned to the deck, and again that same sensation. The sky was now overcast, even though clear weather had been forecast for the following day. That was the first thing I noticed. But I thought, Oh well, the weather will be nice, and if not, it won't matter. In any case, I'd be going home in two and a half months.

I didn't suspect anything. Ignorant. And naive. Incredibly naive. Ralph's letter had arrived two days before: his first letter, after years of silence. In your calm, even hand you had written that you often think of me, that you're looking forward to seeing me again soon. I was flattered. He still thinks of me. I tried reading something more between the lines. Instead of throwing the letter away. But no. It all seemed to be working out well. Suddenly, unexpectedly, there was someone other than my parents waiting for me back home. I wouldn't be alone. It would be easier for me to settle in again; we would go on vacations together, at least for a couple of days, and talk about all the things that had happened in the last few years.

I should have torn up the letter, then and there. But I was curious. How had you changed? And how had I? I wondered if we'd still feel anything for each other. Or would we look at each other like two strangers, desperately trying to conjure up some memories from the past? No. I thought we could start up where we had left off years before, disregarding all that stood between us. Stupid curiosity. And my throat hurt so much, and I didn't want to get sick, and my throat hurt, and I wanted to go swimming, and I thought at worst it might be the flu.

When the ship docked, I went back to the dormitory. And Laura continued the celebration with some of the young men she had met. I felt ill. But I didn't have much to drink, I thought. Why this headache? Why and how come this scratchy throat with no swelling of the glands? Why this feeling that I had to throw up any minute? More and more questions and no answers. No one had an answer. I lay in my bed and couldn't fall asleep, tossing and turning, and many hours later I even heard Laura come in.

In the morning I woke up feeling exhausted. All my joints ached. Still, compulsive as ever, I got up just because I had decided to do so the evening before. I washed, brushed my teeth, and looked at myself in the mirror. I stuck out my tongue but could see nothing unusual in my throat. I took my swimming things and went to the sea. And Laura, fortune's favorite, slept on.

Then I was lying on a blanket at the beach. Wanted to read. But my eyes burned, my head hurt, and I had to move into the shade because I couldn't bear the sun's rays. All around me children were playing, building sandcastles and tunnels. They buried themselves in the sand or threw it at one another. The mothers wore white or colored kerchiefs; the fathers had covered their heads with large newspapers. A beautiful day. It seemed I was the only one who wasn't feeling well. I didn't return to the dormitory until late in the afternoon.

That ugly painted hallway. Staggering along, I saw red and black circles before my eyes, the corridor totally distorted, the walls tilted, the windows slanted. I grabbed at the disgusting, cold walls so as not to lose my balance, to keep from falling. Laboriously, step by step, I groped my way toward the toilet. There I tried to throw up. But nothing came out. I hadn't eaten much so there was only stomach acid, and I spit it out intermittently. I retched and retched. But no relief, no end to it. Merely brief respites that gradually became somewhat longer.

I had heard no news. Not a single news report. I brooded for hours.

Those criminals. Those damned crooks!

Sunstroke, I thought. I really believed I had sunstroke. Never had it before. I had been lying in the shade all day. Sunstroke? Ridiculous. Enough to make you laugh, or cry. Or scream. In a course I had once taken at camp called Basic First-Aid for Young People, we learned: Headache and vomiting in the summertime indicate sunstroke—so rest, lie down, drink liquids, or whatever they told us then. And now nothing else came to mind besides sunstroke. And yet, already in school, during civil defense instruction, I had learned and diligently written down that headache, diarrhea and vomiting, general fatigue with simultaneous sleeplessness, could also be the symptoms of an entirely different sickness. But I had forgotten that long ago. What I had learned in those days had nothing to do with anything we might experience in reality. Had nothing to do with my life. Would never have anything to do with me, I thought.

Laura didn't feel that bad. But then she hadn't been standing up on deck for hours and hours during that night. No. She had been below deck all the time, dancing. She hadn't been lying on the beach all the next day, had been in bed, the windows closed, sleeping off her hangover. Some days later I stood in the rain for hours, not knowing any better, while she sat in a dry dormitory and worried about me. And all this by pure chance, unintentionally, neither of us at fault. She was simply lucky, as always.

Ι

Actually, when was it that I heard about the catastrophe? The first news came from Paul. At the university. On a Monday. As usual he was grinning from ear to ear, coming toward me with bouncy steps, swinging his arms back and forth, angling his elbows exaggeratedly, and alternately lifting his shoulders with each step. What a gawky guy.

I couldn't take him seriously. So on that particular day I tried to steer clear of him, but he headed straight for me. I can still hear his loud voice, his ironic, overbearing tone.

"Well now, did we have a nice weekend? Hear the news? There was a big accident, more than two thousand people dead in a power plant with some strange name about sixty miles from here. I heard it on the radio. As you know, I hear just about everything; I've got my ear to the ground."

I had heard nothing and thought he was showing off. What

kind of accident could that have been? Two thousand dead. In-credible. I shook my head. That couldn't be true.

And he just kept on talking in his supercilious way, "You may as well believe it; it was at a nuclear power plant, if that means anything to you. Your boyfriend studies physics, doesn't he? Per-haps he can give you a little tutoring."

I was angry, could feel myself blushing. How did he know about the letter from Ralph? At that point this was the one thing that concerned me. What business was it of his? And why did he mention it? Somebody must have blabbed. Somebody who knew that Ralph was studying physics. Somebody in our class at school. For the last three years I hadn't said a word about Ralph to any-one. I was furious with Paul; good reason to be on my way.

And later, after I calmed down? Later I thought: Sixty miles away, how can that affect me? What concern is it of mine? I thought. At that time. An accident. A mishap. An explosion. Even if it were true. The people in charge there would surely do what was required. Some of the radio stations probably had an interest in blowing the story out of proportion. I went to a lecture, or to a café or some other place. I don't remember which anymore.

No, I didn't ask anyone whether the place where it happened lay to the north or to the south of Kiev, how far it was from the Kiev Sea, where I had spent that night on the deck of an excur-sion boat. I didn't ask from which direction the wind was blow-ing and I continued to think: Sixty miles, that's a long way off.

I was ignorant, still caught up in traditional concepts of dis-tance; it didn't occur to me that we had long been living in an age when traditional numbers had become meaningless.

Once upon a time, distances between two cities were listed in miles, but that's meaningless today if one doesn't also mention wind direction. Three hundred miles downwind can be equal to less than thirty miles upwind. But the authorities were pretending that twenty miles was still twenty miles. Basta. And this only because it is difficult to evacuate people living in big cities. No, I couldn't have known any better then.

But this apathy. This damned indifference toward everything

that took place anywhere except in my immediate vicinity. This ghastly indifference, the . . .

I just don't understand it. I was incapable of imagining even an iota of what was happening at the accident site at that very moment. Nor did I want to.

My motto was, just don't worry. Don't drive yourself crazy. Don't trouble yourself about things that don't concern you. That's how it was. That's how it is now—yet meanwhile things are happening sixty or six hundred miles away, things that have a direct effect on everyone, as direct as a fire in your own house. But is there anyone who realizes it? Who feels it? Who reacts appropriately?

I

"Yes, I'm really glad you came. Frankly, I've been waiting for you. Once I get started, it seems I have an awful lot to say. Do you mind if I take up your time this way? It doesn't tire me at all. On the contrary, after your last visit I felt relieved and more at ease."

No, that won't do. I won't say anything when he comes. I shouldn't even have started to speak to him. "I'm sorry, but I don't feel like talking. Please respect that."

That's what I'll say when he comes again. Exactly that. Oh, poppycock. Why did I ever agree to see him? No one forced me to. Talking about things will ease your mind, he had said. Nonsense. His questions stirred everything up again. How can all this rehashing of the past and mulling things over be helpful at this point?

I'm no longer interested in any of it!

Still, if it interests him. I have nothing to hide. Actually it doesn't matter. It doesn't matter whether I say anything or not. I don't give a shit. I'm tired. I'm terribly tired.

I couldn't have known better at the time. Really? Wasn't my ignorance a failure on my part? My fault? No. They intentionally kept us in the dark. And yet . . . I should have taken Paul's news more seriously. I could have. Should have. Besides, that same day, or was it the next day . . . ? Anyway, I found out that several students were leaving. Had somebody told me? Laura perhaps? Or did I see the students going to the train station carrying suitcases and bags? I remember only that I noticed: Something's happening. Some students are leaving. But why?

Simply a coincidence, I thought. Didn't I want to make the connection? I would have liked to ask one of them, Where are you going? And why? But I didn't. I knew none of them personally. Sure. They were all students from Western, capitalist countries. Students from Italy, France, Spain, England, etc., with whom we were not allowed to have any contact. And if we did, we had to report, in writing, about each conversation we had with them, each chance encounter. That's why I avoided them. Sure. But was that the real reason? No. I thought: After all, they can travel wherever they want to—and whenever they want to. Besides, I had more important things to do than ask people carrying suitcases where they were going.

But there was this rumor: The roads up north were jammed with cars trying to go south and with army vehicles heading north. Overloaded broken-down old cars were said to be lining the roadsides. Any vehicle that no longer functioned was pushed into a ditch without further ado. Their passengers sought desperately to hitch rides with other people, but that was completely hopeless since all the cars and trucks were jam-packed and overloaded and nobody wanted to stop, make room, and take them along.

I could have followed up on this rumor, could have gone north to see what was going on. Provided I could even have gotten there. Provided all the roads hadn't been closed off. I didn't do it.

And besides, just then the first official news report came out: There had been an accident; two people had died.

There you go, I thought. Two people. Not two thousand. That sort of thing happens from time to time. A train derailment is worse. Even a car accident. No wonder they didn't issue any special news bulletins about such a minor incident. The surprising thing was that the rumors, seemingly without basis in fact, still persisted so stubbornly.

Not only that. They were proliferating. They confused and frightened me. Even though they were much less serious than the truth. But of this truth we knew nothing.

What would I have done in those days had I understood the extent of the catastrophe? Nothing. As an East German I couldn't have left the city. Not legally, that is. I wouldn't have dared to even think of escaping across the border. So I would have had to stay, no matter what. Trapped like a caged animal. Already then, my situation was irreversible and hopeless. Either way. Had I known, fear and the feeling of helplessness would have clawed their way into my brain and my gut that much sooner. At most I might have been somewhat more careful the next few days and in the weeks that followed.

I can still see myself sitting at the table in my room one evening; I open an atlas, measure the distance between two points with a ruler, write the number of inches in the margin of the page, remeasure the distance, and compare it with the first figure in the margin. Unbelievable. A worker in Sweden, six hundred miles to the north, was found to have been exposed to an increased dose of radiation, and the local nuclear reactor was shut down. In Sweden. Another of those rumors. That had to be poppycock. It was beyond belief. Absurd. I slammed the atlas shut with such force that a little cloud of dust whirled up, and replaced it on the shelf. It was all nonsense. And yet, why were children in Poland, just a few hundred miles away, no longer supposed to drink any milk? Why? And why were they distributing iodine tablets on the other side of the border? To protect the thyroid gland? That was all just a lot of talk. All conjecture. A fellow student had told me things while we were passing each other in the hallway, not waiting for my reaction, so I couldn't ask him to tell me more. But I didn't want to ask for more details. I didn't want to know. I didn't believe any of it.

After all, we were much closer to the scene of the accident. Why were no precautions being taken here? No doubt it wasn't necessary. Perhaps the danger existed only at the site itself? It was all nonsense. There was no danger. Or was there? My thoughts circled round and round until I became weary, my eyes closed, and I fell asleep.

The rumors, the news reports we heard, were disjointed, confusing, and contradictory. I couldn't seem to get a clear picture of the situation. The pieces of the puzzle simply didn't fit together. And besides, our usual activities continued right alongside the rumors: lectures, seminars, assemblies, and dancing in the evening. I was caught up in the rhythm of my daily tasks, my little pleasures. They constituted everyday life, led me to believe that everything was normal, and reassured me with false comfort. They refuted the rumors and made them seem completely unreal. Rumors that had to be, could only be, fantasies. Even if from time to time some uncertainty crept in. It was bearable.

Look, what would I have done had I known all about the real state of affairs, the hopelessness of my situation? Would I have gone mad? Would I have . . . already then? I don't know.

My parents tried to reach me by telephone. But they couldn't get through. When they placed the call through a long-distance operator, it was not accepted. They could dial direct, they were told. But whenever they tried, the line seemed to be dead, the call never went through. Finally they called Moscow, which you could still dial direct, and asked some friends to phone me and to tell me I shouldn't eat any fresh fruit or vegetables or drink any milk and to be careful. Days later these friends got through to me, passed along my parents' advice, and said they thought it was all incomprehensible and exaggerated, just as I did. By chance, they had been watching television the evening before, scenes of people in Kiev sunbathing on the beaches. The reporter said life in the city was normal.

Actually, the sun wasn't shining in Kiev at the time, but otherwise I agreed with the television account. I had no inkling that these scenes had been filmed several years ago or why they were being shown now.

I wondered what my parents wanted to warn me against so urgently. How they even knew. After all, they were so far away. Yes, later on everybody knew why they couldn't dial directly, why this old television footage was being broadcast. Later on. But at the time I sat brooding in my room. Till Laura came.

I'd never seen her look like that. Her eyes full of fear. She trembled and whispered even though there was no one else in the room.

"Something's wrong. At the train station. The police are on round-the-clock duty. There's terrible chaos. Everyone who can is leaving. There are fights at the ticket windows. People are offering to pay astronomical amounts of money for tickets. Many don't even bother with tickets, with seats; they simply push their way onto the trains. Children are lifted off the ground and passed along above the heads of the people jammed together on the platform. Even if they themselves can't get away, parents at least want to save their children. They're all crying and shouting. The noise, the frenzy—it's simply unimaginable. Something dreadful must have happened, and somehow it must be connected with the accident, with the catastrophe."

That's when I told you, Laura, about my parents' futile attempts to reach me by telephone and the message they had asked their friends to pass on to me. We looked at each other and hugged, like two people who have to say good-bye forever. You were still trembling. We stood there holding on to each other, both of us thinking: All we can do is wait. Do nothing. Just wait. Wait and wait.

We spent that evening in our room. Tried to find out more from the news broadcasts. Nothing. Later we sat in silence, each bent over a book, both thinking the same thing. Occasionally you looked at me, but I didn't react. I forced myself to stare at my book, at words and letters that made no sense. Whenever I looked up, you were reading or you pretended to be reading.

We went to bed early. We brushed our teeth, undressed, and then lay motionless in our beds. Not a word was spoken. Even though I knew you weren't asleep, and you must surely have known that I couldn't sleep either.

How infinitely long ago all that was.

The next day was May 1. As in other years there was a parade. Thousands, tens of thousands, of people carrying flags, signs, banners, and portraits marched through the streets and past the reviewing stand as though nothing had happened. Everywhere I saw smiling faces, people pressing around colorful stalls that had been built especially for this day. Children riding piggyback on their fathers' shoulders, holding little flags that fluttered in the wind, sucking on candies, licking ice-cream cones. There couldn't have been any real danger. No. Everything was quite normal.

I

One afternoon a few days later I was walking through a quiet, well-tended park on my way from the university to the dorm. Something was moving in the grass, laboriously and awkwardly. At first glance I couldn't tell what it was. I carefully moved closer. It must have been a bird at one time, I thought. That is, it *was* a bird, only it was completely naked, completely bald, had lost almost all its feathers; the two or three drooping feathers that were left seemed so much more grotesque, as though someone had carelessly pasted them on.

I went still closer. Stopped. Never had I seen such a pitiful, ruined creature. The bird was staggering and swaying between the blades of grass, and each blade stood in its path like an insuperable obstacle. I tried to tear my eyes away, wanted to walk on. But as if spellbound I stood there. Transfixed. Motionless. Silent. My mind a blank.

At that moment, the dying bird made everything else around me vanish. The city, the traffic, the university, the dorm. Everything else was wiped from my mind. The bird was all there was.

How precisely I remember it all.

Even then I thought the dying animal was an omen. A warning. A message. Only I couldn't read it, couldn't decipher it. I tried in vain to rid myself of this intrusive notion that seemed so strange and illogical. At last I cried. And yet I had seen dead birds before. At home the cats sometimes caught birds, bit them till they were half dead, and then played with them. That was gruesome, too; it made me sad.

But this was different. This bird was a portent of a disaster that loomed on the horizon but was still invisible.

The thought that someday the same thing that happened to the bird would happen to me flashed through my mind. For some seconds or minutes I became the bird. I saw someone standing over me watching as I lost my last feathers, as I struggled futilely and finally died.

I must have been standing there a long time without realizing it. A storm had gathered. Heavy oily drops rained down. They fell on me and they also hit the bird. It flinched under the raindrops as though they were blows. Then, for quite some time, it remained motionless, twitching less and less often until it just lay there totally still. My hands were trembling as I took my eating utensils out of my briefcase. I dropped the case absentmindedly and, holding firmly on to the handle of the knife, I dug into the ground with hefty stabs. Gradually the soil loosened. I struck a stone, heard a dull metallic sound. Grating against the side of the stone the blade drove farther into the ground. At last the hole seemed deep enough. I tore off a bunch of damp, green grass, spread it out on the black soil in the hollow. Picking up the bird with both hands, I carefully laid it on the bed of grass, covering it with more grass. Then, some loose soil atop the grass and over that the clump of sod I had first dug up. I placed a larger rounded stone over everything. I acted without thinking, unconsciously, following a command no one had given. I had touched the bird with my bare hands, without fear, without the revulsion I normally felt for dead animals.

After that I walked the streets aimlessly. They were deserted, as if the bird had chased away all human beings. Only occasionally did a car or truck drive by. Mostly these were street sprinklers that were now making the rounds in all kinds of weather, at all hours of the day and night. They were supposed to be rinsing away whatever it was that kept coming down from the sky, floating through the air, and, if not inhaled, falling on the roofs, the trees, on the soil, and on the asphalt. But I knew nothing about any of this. It rained and rained; my wet clothes clung to my skin. But I didn't feel anything. I thought about the bird and tried to understand what had happened. All the rumors I had heard raced through my head. Suddenly I panicked and began to mumble to myself: Why are the sprinklers driving through the streets in the rain? Why aren't there any people around? Had the city been abandoned, deserted? What has happened? What caused the bird to die?

I arrived at the dorm thoroughly drenched. It was dark outside. Putting one foot before the other was difficult. Up the stairs. My shoes squished with each step; my hair hung down in wet strands; I was shivering. The hallway seemed endless, getting longer and longer, just as in a nightmare. At last I came to my room and pressed down on the door handle. Locked. I groped for my key, finally found it, dropped my briefcase, unlocked the door, and staggered inside. Without thinking, I threw myself on the bed still wearing all those wet clothes and shut my eyes. I didn't want to see anything, hear anything; it was all too much.

Then Laura came. Hours or minutes later, I don't know. You rushed over to me; your eyes, wide and staring, were filled with shock; you spoke frantic words in a commanding voice; you waved your arms around excitedly. I didn't understand what you were trying to tell me; it was as though you were speaking another language. And even though you were shouting, I could hardly hear you. You were so infinitely far away. I understood nothing you were saying. Wanted to shut my eyes again. Softly, almost in a whisper, I said, "I'm a bird without feathers . . . leave me alone . . . don't yell like that . . . don't touch me . . . you're hurting me . . ."

But you wouldn't stop. Grabbing me roughly, you shook me; you tugged at my clothes. I'd never seen you in such a state. At first, I sat on the edge of the bed, but then I toppled back down again. Not out of ill will. I just didn't have enough strength to sit up. What did it all mean? It was irksome. I wanted you to leave me alone, but again and again you roughly pulled me up, and rapidly and skillfully you undressed me. I watched your nimble hands apathetically. When I was half naked, you suddenly let go of me. Finally, I thought. But in a little while you were back with my bathrobe. With my wet clothes under your arm, my bathrobe slung over your shoulder, you took me by the arm and dragged me down the hall to the shower room. I still didn't know what was going on. But you were so forceful and firm, I no longer resisted. You took off the rest of my clothes, and now I was helping you. Without saying a word but apparently satisfied with what you had accomplished, you pushed me under the shower. The warm water ran over my hair, my skin. It felt good. Slowly I came back to my senses. You handed me some soap and shampoo, having given up trying to explain anything to me. Then you emptied the pockets of my slacks and held the slacks, along with the rest of my clothes, under the shower.

I wanted to protest when you did the same thing to my shoes, but you fended me off. So I watched as the jets of water soaked into my already wet shoes until they looked like sad, scuttled boats. Not until I was back in our room sitting there wrapped in my bathrobe did you explain your peculiar behavior. There had been a public announcement that afternoon—almost two weeks after the catastrophe. Of all times, it came the afternoon I happened to be in the park.

*

DO NOT SPEND MORE TIME OUTSIDE THAN ABSOLUTELY NECESSARY . . .

DO:

KEEP ALL WINDOWS CLOSED . . .

AIR OUT ROOMS BRIEFLY AND ONLY WHEN THE WIND IS BLOWING FROM THE WEST/SOUTHWEST . . .

REMOVE SHOES AND STREETWEAR OUTSIDE YOUR APARTMENT . . .

KEEP GROCERIES IN CLOSED CONTAINERS . . .

DAMP-MOP THE FLOORS EVERY DAY . . .

DUST ONLY WITH A DAMP RAG . . .

KEEP PETS INDOORS . . .
SHOWER AT LEAST TWICE A DAY . . .
WASH YOUR HAIR EVERY DAY . . .
LISTEN TO NEWS REPORTS REGULARLY . . .

I

You did exactly the right thing by tearing my clothes off. You asked where I had been that afternoon, and I told you about the bird. You didn't think I was crazy. I can still hear you saying, "That's really a sad story, but you ought to take better care of yourself and not be so foolish as to stay outside so long, especially when it's raining."

Yes, if I hadn't been out in the rain for such a long time, if I hadn't sailed about on the Kiev Sea on that excursion boat, getting ever closer to the accident site, if I hadn't been at the beach all day . . . if . . . if . . . if . . . But I did. Because I didn't know. Because up to that point no one knew.

Then you told me you'd gone to the store and bought a few cans of fish, some jars of jam, and several packages of crackers and cookies. A few hours later there were no packaged goods left in the stores. But then, you were always in the right place at the right time. You tried to cheer me up. Telling me about the man who tried to grab your shopping bag as you were coming out of the store. You acted out how you tugged and pulled, called for help, and then swore at him. He was flabbergasted.

And I had to laugh when you imitated him waddling off with his fat belly, quite distraught. Then we both went to sleep. It was warm in the room, but we didn't open the window. There was a light breeze from the northwest.

A few days later all the children were loaded into trucks and buses and driven south, away from the city. There were scenes I had seen in war movies: a jumble of bundles, bags, and suitcases of all possible shapes and colors; the thin arms of little children tightly clasping their mothers' necks, tears, a frantic running to and fro, arguments because some of the children had more baggage than was permitted. Then handkerchiefs were waving in the wind, and the chaperones accompanying the children tried to comfort them as best they could.

The city was without children. For a time it was easy to ignore that. But then I noticed a difference in the mood of the people on the buses, on the streets, in the parks I hurried through, in the squares I hastily crossed. No ball playing, no tussling, no laughter, no crying. No little ones needing a comforting hand. No one reaching for the candies I carried in my pockets. The playgrounds were deserted.

I

It was late by the time we began to occupy ourselves with measurements, conversion factors, and the biological effects of radioactive particles. Suddenly references to elements from the Periodic Table that I had learned about in school popped up in discussions everywhere. Only now they were furnished with unconventional numbers, had unbelievable half-lives ranging anywhere from seconds to twenty-four thousand years. A lot of things were still confusing. There would be announcements saying: "Caution! The radiation intensity is very high," then shortly afterward came the reassuring message, "The biological effect is minimal." If the biological effect was high, they said, "The intensity of radiation is low." But if both were high, they said, "The half-life is only hours or days; there is no danger." It was extraordinary! Always some consolation. No matter what, the situation was never dangerous, never hopeless. We were always lucky. And I was naive enough to believe it. What's more, it wasn't at all hard to believe.

No one mentioned the exponential nature of the danger, or the cumulative risks, the long-term effects, the influence of low-level radiation dosages on the human organism; nor did they talk about the food chain and radioactive accumulations in the soil.

It was much too late by the time we finally asked ourselves where the food we ate was coming from. Which food items were more contaminated and which less so. And how one could find out. No one knew. What was in the water we showered with? No one knew. Some of my fellow students thought that taking showers would reduce the surface radioactivity; others claimed that showering would open our pores and the radioactive particles would then be able to enter the body more easily. A few recommended wearing a dampened face mask, but public officials prohibited us from doing that, saying it would cause panic. I would have gone mad if I had tried to follow all the advice and recommendations.

And besides, right alongside all this chaos of contradictory advice and information, our everyday life, the normal school routine—the lectures, studying for exams, and writing papers—simply continued as usual.

Sometimes I wondered: Why should I go on taking exams and writing papers while my health, my life, are already at risk—the air, the water, the food, contaminated by radiation? Does it make any sense? At such times I felt as though I were walking a tightrope stretched over a deep abyss. It was as though I were paralyzed. I had to catch my breath with every move I made. Each day, every hour, whatever I did became agony.

At other times I would tell myself: No! Don't do this to yourself. You have to finish your studies; that's your assignment, your duty, the one thing that's a constant. This jumble, this confusion of reports and opinions, will pass; someday the situation will change, but you'll always have your degree.

Thinking along these lines, I would pretend that the abyss didn't exist, and I felt better about what was happening.

My ignorance helped me to adjust. Somehow everything became bearable. Became only transitional. Became easy. I felt as if I were participating in a civil defense drill.

The entire city was practicing how to behave in case of radioactive fallout, except that they were all behaving as though it were the real thing. Yet, the whole operation was just a game in which you obeyed the rules, more or less. After all, it didn't really matter how the game would end.

It's incredible how careless we became. We no longer mopped the floors or dusted as often. We didn't shower as frequently. I scarcely noticed the people who were holding Geiger counters over crates of fruits and vegetables, even when the instruments chattered like toy guns.

I can still remember what I thought at the time: Sooner or later the drill will have to be called off. It must come to an end sometime. This can't go on forever. It's becoming absurd, grotesque.

Couldn't the children come back now—with red cheeks and happy faces, just as though they'd been on vacation or at camp or had a few days off from school because of a heat wave? Sometime soon the authorities will have to announce that people can keep their shoes on when they enter their apartments, that they can drop this onerous hairwashing, especially since we haven't been able to get shampoo for a while. Then, at long last, we'll be able to go swimming again and sit on a park bench in the late afternoon sun and eat fresh fruits and vegetables, too. But the drill simply didn't stop. It went on and on and on.

⁞

When I try to understand it all, here and now lying in this bed—it's completely incomprehensible to me. Even though it concerned us directly, even though the calamity had caught up with us and the situation had long since become serious, we had—I had—denied it. Not an entirely conscious process. There was too much that I heard and actually experienced daily for that to be possible. But again and again I gave the facts an innocuous twist. Suppressed them. And all those around me did the same. That way we cheered each other up. We had practiced for the real thing so often, and yet it never did get serious.

Was this suppression of reality also a defense mechanism to keep from going crazy? Perhaps, subconsciously, one hoped to come to terms with the disaster by denying it ever happened, denying it to oneself and in front of others? One pretends to be ignorant. One plays dead. Just like some animals play dead in threatening situations. I can't explain my apathy in those days in any other way.

Of course, over the years we had become accustomed to having the true state of affairs concealed from us. Things were glossed over; crises and disasters were covered up with reassuring words and official platitudes. We were supposed to learn how to overcome our problems by ignoring them. And we became good at it. We learned to see anyone who faced the facts, who called a spade a spade, who destroyed our web of deception and self-deception, as the enemy.

I

I had also become numb through force of habit. Soon it was difficult to imagine that only a short while ago I had gone on walks through the city or on long hikes through the woods near Kiev without a second thought. Of course, I still remembered and hadn't lost my yearning for those walks, but I resigned myself to the new situation surprisingly quickly. Staying in closed rooms seemed as normal and natural as walking outdoors had been.

Except gradually I felt a tension growing within me, an undefinable discontent, and then some trivial thing would trigger an outburst against Laura or whoever was nearby. That never used to happen before. I also felt tired, unspeakably tired. As though I would never be able to get enough sleep.

Yet, I slept twelve hours a day, often lay down right after class. And never felt like getting up, either in the morning or in the afternoon. I was plagued by a lack of appetite. When other students came to our room to talk, I sat there apathetically as though none of it concerned me. Every day I heard about people who had committed suicide. I didn't believe the rumors, or I thought that this sort of thing happens all the time; it's just that now they're paying special attention to these things. But even when the reports were substantiated, they had surprisingly little impact on me.

This apathy should have been an omen for me. How shocked I used to be whenever I heard that someone had committed suicide. I would wonder whether something could have been done to help, whether the poor soul had any friends. Always I would think about how much he or she would be missing. And now I almost envied those people: They were lucky. They can sleep now, sleep all the time, and no one will ever wake them up.

I

So it had already begun at that time. At that time I . . . Right. For the first time. This insight was the first step. My very first. Ah, but no, at times I resisted understanding.

When they told us about an old woman who had thrown herself in front of a street sprinkler, I burst out, "But that's stupid. The driver was only doing his job. He's doing it for everyone's good. It cuts down on the radiation. Why jump in front of a sprinkler? You get flushed away by the water, and then a car might hit you, and that driver really doesn't have the slightest connection to any of this. None. None at all. Oh, stop blabbering all of you; it's unbearable! How am I supposed to concentrate on preparing for my exams with all this noise!" And then I threw myself on my bed and put my hands over my ears. And Laura came over and patted me on the back.

I

We were among the very last to leave. All the other foreign students, even those from Hungary, Poland, and Czechoslovakia, had moved up the dates for their examinations and had gone home early. Only the GDR students stayed on.

Paul and I, of all people, were chosen to go to the GDR Consulate. Why pick me? Why Paul? In the name of the students of . . . What a laugh! It took forever before we could get an appointment.

Soft chairs, coffee, cigarettes, and then they urged us to speak freely about our problems. Paul started. He really did the best he could. If I had tried that, I couldn't have gotten a word out. I was surprised how calmly and confidently he spoke in the face of the stiff smile on the consular official's face. Even though he knew that every one of his words was being taken down by a diligent secretary who refilled the coffee cups only when the official was talking.

"In short," Paul continued, warming to his subject, "we also insist that our examinations be given at an earlier date so that we can finish the semester sooner. We've prepared a detailed schedule; we thought this is how it can be done."

Thought nothing. Thought out. Finished thinking. The consulate official held up both his hands, palms out, to cut him off.

I'll never forget how Paul was struck dumb. He kept moving his lips, kept speaking even after the official's demand for silence, arduously formulating sentence after sentence. But no words came out of his mouth. No sound in the room except the regular ticking of a clock. It took forever until Paul noticed. Startled, he finally stopped shaping his futile silent phrases.

The official seemed to have been waiting for this. He inclined his head slightly as though he were thinking something over, and then he began with the royal "we."

"We can understand that you have misgivings and are worried. We accept that, and we think it's a good thing that you have spoken so frankly about it. Mutual trust is an important prerequisite for solving problems jointly. But I would like to ask that you try to understand our position as well. Precisely in this difficult and complex situation it is necessary to show one's solidarity with one's hosts. Look. The people who live here can't just drop everything and simply take off. In addition, finishing your school year, or your studies, early would be like sending a signal to them. You noticed how the premature departure of students from other countries aroused a certain disquiet and apprehension. Just so that there will be no misunderstanding, I want to emphasize that I don't wish to get mixed up in the affairs of other countries; they can make their own decisions about their citizens. But it is important that there be no panic. That everything proceed as normally as possible.

"Therefore," he continued after a brief pause, "I would like to appeal to your sense of responsibility to help us cope with this difficult situation. Look here," he lowered his voice confidentially, "this isn't easy for me either. You'll be leaving in a few weeks, no matter what. But our work here goes on. So, please complete your studies successfully, prove yourselves worthy of the hospitality provided to you here, and tell your fellow students about what I said. If there are any further problems, you're welcome to come to see me again."

I keep hearing his voice, those friendly, threatening words. Even here, even now. That was a year ago. Won't I ever be able to keep the sound of that voice from going round and round in my head?

No one drank any more coffee. The rest of the cigarettes remained unsmoked. I still see him bouncing out of his chair as though he wanted to demonstrate to us how physically fit he was. We had no choice but to get up, too. He had clasped his hands and moved them up and down in front of his chest as though he were standing on a reviewing stand, performing a symbolic handshake for the people marching by. But he just wanted to urge us to be reasonable at last, and to leave.

"Thanks very much for talking with us," Paul said sarcastically. But the official ignored him and said, "Yes, you're welcome, no problem. Good luck with your exams." And with that we were pushed out of the room.

I

I felt awful. Had I even said as much as a whole sentence? They should have sent someone else. When we returned to the dorm, all eyes were on us.

As though by prearrangement, we shrugged our shoulders simultaneously. Paul flicked his hands twice as though he wanted to get rid of some invisible dirt that clung to his fingers.

And then the inevitable question. "Didn't you accomplish *anything?*" And Paul's laconic reply, "Yes, we did; we don't have to stay any longer than originally scheduled. We have to be considerate of our hosts."

Some of the students swore. Others wept. One said, "I told you from the start it made no sense to go over there." We were left with fatalism, resignation, weariness. To be followed by nightmares.

Up to then, I had hardly ever paid attention to my dreams. If

I remembered anything at all about them the next morning, I quickly forgot. It was in Kiev that I first began to understand what dreams are about. They give expression to things that are not allowed to push their way into one's consciousness during the day. Dreams . . .

A dark night. Crooked streets. An old town. Arrows. Pin-sized arrows. They glow yellow, red, violet. Driven by the wind. They penetrate things. So quick, so swift. Put your hands over your face! They go right through the hands. Pierce my eyes. Are inside my head.

Ahead, a brightly lit palace. A black iron gate. Open. But first I have to cross this huge, empty square. I have to reach the palace. The arrows become more and more painful. Keep going. Keep going. Finally a small door. Locked. Pound on it. With my fists. It opens a crack. A man. He looks like a chauffeur or a servant in an old English film. In tails and a top hat. What is he saying?

"Would you like anything else, milady?" Is he mad? He indicates that I'm supposed to follow him. We are no longer outside. Finally some protection from the arrows. Why should I undress? It's cold here. No windows in this room. At least he's not watching me. Now he gestures. Where are we going? Everything is tiled. Yellowed. Where is he taking me? A padded door opens. And is closed behind me.

I'm alone. A desk in front of me. A single sheet of paper on it. White. Blank.

Behind the desk, only vague silhouettes. Light and dark spots. Tones of gray. A figure, a man. I don't know him. Instead of a nose he has the hooked beak of a bird of prey. His fingers terminate in sharp claws. The birdman looks at me.

I am naked. I cover my breasts with my right arm, hold my left hand over my crotch. Now he opens his beak. Makes croaking sounds. What is he saying?

I'm to come closer. Still closer. Don't be so timid. What are you doing here? I have no idea. I try to say, "I want to leave this place." But what's the matter with my tongue? It's so thick; so swollen. I hear myself saying, "I want to leave this place; the arrows are going to kill me!" Did I say that? Yes, I said it. Finally his beak moves.

"Could do. Would be pleased to do. Fill out form. Fill out form." One of his claws pushes the piece of paper toward me. It is smeared with blood. "Do nothing. Do nothing." The beaked head moves back and forth, left, right, left, right. First one eye looks at me, then the other. The birdman flaps his wings. I flinch. But he veers off, toward the window. A piercing scream. Shattered glass falls tinkling to the ground. The creature disappears in the distance. Getting smaller and smaller.

The birdman's suit lies on the chair. On the desk, the blood-smeared paper. Carefully I take it, fold it. I run off. Up a down escalator. Still naked. Along a deserted train platform, running after a departing train. And the distance between me and the train becomes ever greater.

Where am I? Damned dream. Please don't let me have these terrible dreams again. Please. I must have fallen asleep. I'm exhausted. I can't go on. I don't want to go on. When will I ever again be able to sleep without having dreams?

If the pastor comes back, I'll throw him out. All that jabbering. My life is at an end. Finished. Over. Let him leave me alone. Let them all leave me alone. All of them. Who cares anyway? No one. No one. Get that into your head. It's ridiculous to think, to talk about it anymore. After he goes home, I'll have more nightmares. No, thank you. I won't play that game any longer.

The rivers stink; we don't smell it. The fish are dying. The trees wither in the acid rain. We can see it happening every day. If we want to. But we refuse to look.

Who is going to defend himself against something that approaches invisibly? Soundlessly? That can neither be smelled nor felt? Nobody. Until it's too late. I didn't defend myself. I denied it.

Repressed it as long as I could. Wanted to escape. To forget. Instead I did nothing. Nothing. What could I have done? It's all so useless. Doesn't matter whether I protest or whether I am silent, whether I rebel. Against whom, actually? It's all absurd. Let them put me in the booby hatch. Radiation phobia. The end. Finis.

Ah, yes. If fifty thousand inhabitants of a city were to die in one week, then perhaps people would sit up and take notice. Perhaps. But this way, each person dies by himself. His own lonely death. Alone. And nothing need be verified. To anyone. Anyway, to whom? And why? Who can know how old she might have become? What course might her life have taken had she not been exposed to radiation? Would she have lived another ten, twenty, even thirty years? Would she have had children? Healthy children? Healthy grandchildren? Would she not have been infertile? Would cancer not have consumed her? Or would leukemia not have struck her down?

Uncounted numbers of people die silently. Nameless victims vanish. Reappear only as statistics. The frequency of fatal cancers is x percent higher than the yearly average of . . . And even the statistics are kept secret. There must be no panic. Just keep going. Don't draw any obvious conclusions. A dead man doesn't talk. A dead woman doesn't talk. And they both die in their hospital beds and accept it as their personal fate.

Has no one realized we have been designated as the victims, that in the course of this large-scale experiment we are nothing but objects to be dealt with in any way they see fit? Why don't any of those who have been poisoned, contaminated by radiation, set themselves on fire in front of a nuclear power plant? Why do we all die so quietly, so secretly, from the fire burning within us? Why?

I

I am upset. After all, what did I do? Nothing. Absolutely nothing. And what could I have done? Put up placards? Enlighten the masses? Others have already tried that. Join some ecology group in its discussions? What can possibly be accomplished? It's like preaching to the converted: The only people you convince are those who are already convinced. The ignorant will remain ignorant. Those who believe in progress will go on believing in it.

No, I'll go quietly, steal away rather than go on—like so many others—tottering through hospital corridors on crutches of hope.

No. I don't want to deceive myself, to conceal the real reality from myself.

We have been burnt by "peaceful" atoms, we have been burnt from within. We are the slaves of modern times, condemned to die so that everything will go on as before. The military maneuvers, the wasteful consumption of electricity, the commercial neon signs.

The firemen, the cleanup squads, they are the gladiators of the modern era. They were sent to their death. Had they not gone into the reactor plant, half of Europe would now be uninhabitable. Farewell to the Western world. Farewell to European civilization. They sacrificed themselves. Their sacrifice was in vain.

They obtained a grace period for us, but it led nowhere. We learn nothing, draw no obvious conclusions. And those who gave them the orders to die, to die in installments, now order us to carry on; while they still sit up on the reviewing stand, far away.

"We assume the responsibility. It has been scientifically shown that . . ."

And whom can the unborn children accuse? And when should they do it? Before which court? Who will take "responsibility" for what happened and is still happening at the site of the disaster? And soon will happen elsewhere? No one. No political party. No corporation. No country. No one. Responsibility. Responsibility. What a stupid old word. Meaningless in a catastrophe of such magnitude. To do something. But what? What?

❚

When he gets here, I'll say, "Reverend," I'll say, "your Lord Jesus has been dead for two thousand years. A paltry two thousand years. But the bones of those poisoned by radioactivity will still be radiating after *twenty-four* thousand years—twelve times as long as your entire Christian history. Your so-called Christian calendar. By then, no one will be thinking of me any longer. But

I, too, will continue to radiate, on and on. That is the modern form of resurrection. The Word simply hasn't gotten around yet." That's what I'll say to him.

Oh, do I really want to rage like this, rail at him, and insult him? He's taking the time to listen to my speeches, to my questions, to the insight that has come too late. Can't he understand that it is hopeless? For me. With me. For us all?

He will again plump up my pillow, look at me for a long time, and say nothing. Until I go on talking.

I could tell him about my dreams, about the red and green arrows that bore through me while I sleep. But what for? I could tell him how foolish it is to take university exams seriously.

I

How I worried about those examinations, whether I would pass, and how well I would do! Not one of the exams was rescheduled for an earlier date. They dragged on for weeks. But it never occurred to me to wonder why I was still taking them.

Not until we had to report for our final physical examination—normally a routine affair. That's when I first began to feel real fear.

It gripped me suddenly, insinuated itself under my skin, dug its claws into my brain. I was trembling. What if they find something? What if they find something wrong *with me*?

Blood tests, urine analysis, questions. Then all the results were in, compiled. The final interview. Three doctors sitting behind an oval table covered with piles of papers. They looked tired, exhausted. I can still see the gray-haired man who sat in the middle, exactly as he looked then. He had a furrowed face and heavy bags under his eyes. He was older than the other two and did all the talking. He held his head a little to one side and looked directly at me as he spoke. His voice was friendly and quite calm.

"According to the test results, your general physical condition is satisfactory. But we can tell you practically nothing about the aspect that must surely be of greatest concern to you. The actual amount of radiation exposure for individuals can only be approximately and indirectly determined. I am sure you know that in addition to the total dose of radiation, many other factors are involved. It depends on how the radioactive particles were absorbed, where they subsequently became concentrated, the size of the affected organ, and so on."

Then he asked me where I had been during the time of the disaster and in the days that followed, whether I had been aware of any unusual symptoms.

I told him about the cruise on the boat, my sunbathing the next day, and how I felt afterward. Also, that at the time I thought I had had sunstroke. I mentioned my lengthy walk in the rain, and I said I constantly felt tired.

From time to time, while I was speaking, he would exchange brief glances with the other doctors. He wanted to know how closely I had later adhered to the rules that were issued.

"At the beginning, very closely; later, I became more careless."

He nodded, looked down at his hands, and sighed.

"Yes," he said after a long pause. Just that one word. Then silence. It seemed as though he had to pull himself together before he could continue.

"Hardly anyone recognized the dangers and their full scope in time. And the response was correspondingly late and contradictory. No one was up to the tremendous responsibility. Perhaps this responsibility exceeded human capabilities, the capacity of the human imagination. We, as doctors, deal with individual cases only and are powerless. Nevertheless, you should have observed the instructions issued after the disaster more strictly. I don't want to hide from you the fact that we cannot precisely measure or treat absorbed radiation, and certainly we cannot reduce or neutralize it. We are powerless against the demons humankind has loosed, and no master magician will come to our aid at the last moment. Our medical prognoses can only be vague; we have but scant experience with low- and medium-size doses of radiation, their potentiation, and their multiple effects on the human organism. To be on the safe side, I would recommend that you not think of having children in the next few years."

Yes. He used exactly those words. In that tone of voice. Very softly.

And I asked naively, without even comprehending the implications of his and my words, "What do you mean 'in the next few years'? What do you mean by 'recommend'?"

Again he hesitated before answering, "In the next ten years. But, as I emphasized before, this is a recommendation. Only a recommendation."

You were right in your recommendation, Doctor. More than right.

Then he got up, looking as though it cost him great effort. He was much shorter than I had thought. He was still looking directly into my eyes, but I had the feeling he no longer saw me, that he was gazing at something immeasurably far away. Perhaps he had a premonition.

He stood there as though he were carrying a heavy burden, not quite certain that he would ever arrive with it at his destination. With his slender hand he tightly grasped mine: "I wish you all the best in the future, all the best."

Your good wishes didn't help, Doctor. They didn't help at all.

I nodded briefly, turned, and quickly walked out. Then I cried. The sort of crying during which a bottomless pit yawns before you; you are alone in the world and feel lost. Once again I thought of the bird. Suddenly everything had become clear.

Much as a blinding lightning flash in the dark of night allows you to see a landscape you could only guess at before, I knew at that moment—clearly, as never before or ever again—what had happened in the last two and a half months. But just as the flash of lightning lasts only an instant, and everything that has become visible again vanishes into the darkness, so my clear view of things was brief.

After all, I had to pack and send off my things, had to fill out customs declarations, register my departure with the appropriate authorities, take care of endless errands, often more than once. On top of that, I had to go to this macabre meeting. Participation was mandatory. The things I put up with.

The room was packed, the air stuffy. I thought about everything I still had to do; nonetheless, I listened to that boring, long-winded voice. I didn't jump to my feet. Didn't interrupt, didn't shout, "Do you know what a doctor told me a few days ago?" No. I didn't even run out of the room. I sat there and listened to it all until the end.

"In our country, scientific technical progress is not an end in itself. Rather, it is subordinated to the greater goal of serving the welfare of the people. Of course, our enemies will try to take advantage of this accident—you already know all about that—to serve their own selfish interests." And so on and so forth.

Then he recited a series of names and dates. There had been accidents and mishaps in nuclear power plants in other countries during the last few decades, he said. In these safe nuclear power plants that posed no danger. And for decades the information about such accidents had been kept concealed. Of course, all this was attributable only to the greed for profit. Under no circumstances was nuclear energy, in and of itself, to be called into question. No.

"The question always comes down to this: Who is making use of the technology in whose interest?" Why didn't I laugh? If only he would stop. Stop. That damned voice droning on and on.

"Basically, what differentiates us is the way our people behave in such a difficult situation. Tens of thousands of families have taken children into their homes; food packages have been sent; many generous donations have been received; and countless numbers of people have volunteered for deployment in the 'temporarily contaminated areas.'"

Ghost towns. Dead villages. Contaminated countryside. Homelands now lost to hundreds of thousands of people.

"Only when you contemplate the contextual whole, rather than arbitrarily selecting single occurrences, can you form a realistic overall picture. One has to see the problem in all its complexity and manifold aspects to be able to deal with it in a responsible manner and to counteract panic mongering and technophobia.

"This is precisely what I would ask of you as well-educated

young people, especially once you start your homeward journeys. No matter who speaks to you about what happened here. Everything always depends on the point of view from which you describe things.

"You must restrain yourselves particularly in the presence of citizens from other countries. Personally I have faith in you, and I think you will justify this faith."

And then we were supposed to sign a statement saying we had been properly briefed. Briefed. Only later did this turn into a pledge of secrecy. I sat there the entire time holding a pencil, a sheet of paper in front of me, and when he stopped talking, I looked at the paper. Many little crosses, each with a long vertical post and a short horizontal crossbar, were drawn all over the sheet. I quickly folded the paper. Fear. Always this vague fear that made me wrap myself in silence, caused me to sit still, to listen, to be submissive.

A few days later we left. I wasn't happy. At least not in the way I had been imagining it for days and weeks. I had walked through the streets of Kiev wistfully, tried to memorize the gestures and faces of the people, how they spoke, how they behaved toward one another.

Worst of all was saying good-bye to Laura. We both cried; our hands touched. Hardly had we taken a few steps away from each other when we ran back again. And so we vacillated, back and forth. Invisible threads seemed to keep me from leaving you. Finally, with quick, firm steps, you left. I watched you until you disappeared in the crowd without once having turned around.

And then I stood there. Alone with my fear, my uncertainty about what was to come. Later, I forgot you. Erased you from my life. At that moment, had anyone told me this would happen, I would not have believed it, would never have thought it possible.

Pictures. Sounds. Once again I was sitting in an airplane. I thought back to that first flight to Kiev. How long ago was that? The time interval seemed short, like a dream. It also seemed incredibly long. Was I still the girl who had just graduated from high school and was now leaving her parents, flying to an unknown, far-off land? Had I matured? Was I older? A different person? How was I different from my earlier self? In what respect had I remained true to myself? Who was I? There was a degree in my briefcase. Five winters and summers had come and gone. And now? I hunted for my pocket mirror. My face was more womanly, more mature, no longer so childishly curious. Would Ralph still like me? How had he changed in the meantime? Would he come to the airport to pick me up? All this was so terribly important. Then.

I was still immersed in thought when they announced we were landing. Once the plane came to a halt I couldn't wait to get to the exit, down the gangway, through passport control. I waited impatiently for the baggage, finally found my suitcase, quickly grabbed it, went through the gate, and looked around, searching.

Mother came hurrying toward me. I saw her face, her questioning eyes, the wrinkles, the strands of gray in her hair. Her lips kept forming the same words over and over, "My child, my child, my child." Father joined us and laid one of his big hands on my shoulder.

I was only dimly aware of what was going on around me, as though I were hearing and seeing it through a veil. It was all muted, merely a humming, a buzzing. Slowly the noises became louder, the fragments of words comprehensible. There was incredulity, disbelief on the faces of those waiting, as though I and those who had come through the door before or after me had not been expected to return alive. I had the same feeling an ocean voyager must have when he reaches land a long time after his ship has been reported sunk. And yet, it seemed then that everything was still possible for me. Salvation. Hope. A new beginning.

Ralph was standing there. Was it really Ralph? This man with the dark beard, squeezed into a jacket, holding a bunch of flowers?

But you recognized me, came toward me, embraced me, kissed me on the cheek, handed me the flowers which gave off an overpowering fragrance. You recognized me. That was like a bridge between the before and after. Therefore nothing insuperable could have happened. I couldn't have changed fundamentally. Your presence was a consolation.

"Well, let's go," I heard Father say. He picked up one of my suitcases, Ralph the other. Mother took my arm, and we walked to the car. It was drizzling. The windshield wipers left a smeary film on the glass. The streets, houses, and squares went by as if in a motion picture. I saw that here and there a new store had opened or a house had been painted. But the city seemed strange. I waited to see a building, a café, a street where I would suddenly feel: I'm home. But there was no feeling of happiness. Everything remained unfriendly and cold.

How could life have continued here as though nothing special had happened? And what business did I have here, I who had come from another world and had somehow happened upon this place by mistake? But then I felt Ralph's hand. It was like a life preserver for me, an assurance: You're really here. It isn't just a dream.

The film kept rolling. Father stopped the car. Ralph got out and opened the garden gate. Father drove up to the front door. Mother and I got out. Carefully I placed one foot in front of the other; I was afraid the ground might suddenly vanish before me, open up, give way, and I would plunge into the yawning abyss, into nothingness.

But the earth sustained me, the stairs bore up under me. Mother's key fit the lock, the door to the beautiful house allowed itself to be opened. One miracle after another. The walls did not crash down upon me. I went into the bathroom and carefully turned on a faucet.

Water actually came pouring out; I could see it, feel it on my skin. Still skeptical, I continued to collect evidence of my being in this place.

I washed my hands, rinsed my face with cold water, rubbed

a hopeful glow into my face with the towel. The mirror did not disappoint me. Then I looked around the bathroom: new hooks on the walls, new curtains at the windows, the old familiar laundry hanging on the clothesline.

There was music coming from downstairs. Mother was playing the piano. A familiar piece by Mozart. She used to play it often; I knew every note. Quietly I opened the bathroom door to hear better, to take in the sound. But as I listened more carefully, I suddenly began to doubt whether it was really Mother who was playing. The notes were right; she didn't make a single mistake, didn't get stuck even once, but this was subtly different from her former playing. It was as though the notes occasionally were reluctant to leave the piano; at other times they seemed to be chasing one another with unseemly haste, almost tumbling over one another. There was an element of nervous excitement and insistence in this music that frightened me.

The rift that went through my very being was already anticipated, was already audible in her playing. It was as if, when you're clinking glasses, one of them doesn't ring clear. You can tell that it has a crack, even if you can't yet see it.

I hesitantly walked down the hall to the music room. The door was slightly ajar, and I looked inside. Father and Ralph were standing there, halfway between Mother and the partially open door through which I would enter.

The piece was finished. I stepped through the door. Father and Ralph applauded; Mother turned around. All three looked at me. On the coffee table were Ralph's flowers and a lit candle; there were also little packages wrapped with carefully tied ribbons. Through the half-open window I heard birds twittering; the rain had stopped. Dust motes danced in a slender ray of sunshine that fell into the room. Everything had been prepared so carefully, and I, I became afraid. I rushed over to the window, pushed the curtains out of the way, and slammed it shut. Then I stopped, rooted to the spot. One could probably leave the windows open here. I turned around and looked at them apologetically. But no one seemed to have noticed.

Father said, "Welcome home again, and congratulations on getting your degree." Mother and Ralph also congratulated me. I thanked them, and timidly I embraced all three, one after the other. Father and Ralph were getting along naturally and casually. I intended to inquire later about their grand, amicable entente, but I was much too preoccupied with myself.

Mother said we should go into the living room for coffee and cake. As I walked in, the first thing I saw was the picture of the ballet dancer spinning on her own axis like a crazy woman. She exerted a strong pull, and I couldn't take my eyes off her. Then everything went black. Holding on to the back of a chair, I thought: You're about to fall down, ballerina. After that I don't remember a thing.

I awoke in bed, upstairs in my room. It was dark outside. I stared at the ceiling. You're home again, I thought. Everything will be all right now; a new chapter in your life is about to begin. Someone was coming up the stairs. I quickly closed my eyes. It was you, Mother. You put your cool hand on my forehead, but I pretended to be asleep. You stood next to my bed for a long while; I could scarcely hear you breathe. What were you thinking? What could have been going through your mind? Were you remembering scenes from my childhood? Or were you simply happy I was back? You closed the door gently and went back downstairs, groping for each step as though you were in the dark or, like an old woman, unsteady on your feet.

I turned back the blanket carefully, got up, and hesitantly, softly, walked over to the window. There was a full moon. A milky gray suffused the garden; the trees were black and still, casting long shadows. Everything will be all right, I thought; everything will be all right. After all, it was only *a recommendation.* Only a recommendation, a suggestion.

I was in bed for three or four days with a low-grade fever; I felt weak. Ralph came to see me every day. He would sit down on a chair next to my bed, sometimes touching me as if by accident, and I was pleased to have him do that.

I thought of the time we were studying for the exams and I

had surreptitiously observed his hands. Now he brought me things to drink, plumped up my pillow, and picked out a record to play. Without my having to tell him, he sensed when I wanted to be by myself. Soon I was able to get up. Again he was there. While I dressed, he made coffee and set the breakfast table outside in the garden. In the garden.

You brought out the blue coffee pot, put fresh rolls next to it; you even found the jam and honey. You knew where everything was kept. Everything you did was so matter-of-fact, as though you had been living in our house for a long time. Eating breakfast outside in the garden . . . that was paradise.

The past was behind us. We talked only about the future. Made plans. Something new had begun, and we wanted to shape it. We spent whole days together. One evening you stayed over. We drank wine; a candle flickered near the open window; melted wax ran down one side, drop by drop, solidified halfway down, and formed a blob that got bigger and bigger. We listened to the Canadian singer Leonard Cohen. His voice prompted me to daydream; it suggested the security I so often had sought but not found.

We lay on my bed, naked, talking, smoking, drinking wine. I can still feel the round porcelain ashtray you placed on my stomach. It was cool, and I warmed it with my skin. Soon I no longer felt it at all. I followed the two small red dots that floated through the dark room, coming toward each other and then separating again. Your face became a reddish silhouette whenever you dragged deeply on your cigarette. I couldn't see the ash in the ashtray on my belly.

I dipped my finger into the wine and very carefully drew lines and dots on your face: "Nice that you are here." You couldn't read that. Then I removed the ashtray from my stomach and kissed off the words I had written on your skin.

I

You were just what I needed. Then. I didn't care how things had gone with your last girlfriend. We needed each other. I got completely caught up in our relationship, used it to distract myself, and thought I was incredibly happy.

I was glad to be home again, in my room where nothing had changed in the last few years, except for a few plants that had grown larger and some new ones Mother had added. And you were there again.

I pretended that the last five years had never happened, that I had just graduated from high school. How happy I felt in my fantasy. The illusions of happiness and a new beginning came easily, and I grasped at them only too gladly.

In the days before I left—actually, had I ever left?—I wanted to have a child. But I needn't have left at all. No. I can pick up exactly at the point at which, then, out of cowardice, I decided not to follow my instinct. Then? What do I mean by "then"? It was just a short while ago. A few days ago. Just now. I never made the wrong decision. I never left at all.

It was all so simple, so obvious. And you, Doctor, you were so far away—*only a recommendation.* It wasn't just six hundred miles, or just ten years. No. You spoke to me in another life. Only a recommendation. No disaster had befallen me. Not me.

I had been back ten days, and I felt like a new woman. I was living in a new world, speaking another language, at home again. I was sure I had been lucky. No doubt about it.

I threw myself at you like a Fury. Poor Ralph. I used you; I was so uninhibited, driven by a madness about which you couldn't have had a clue. I scarcely recognized myself. To have a child. With a recommendation. Without a recommendation. To have a child. I was mad. I simply didn't want to believe what had happened to me. That I had been exposed to radiation. Me, not someone else.

I denied it. Spun a cocoon of denial around myself. The doctor could have made a mistake. After all, what is a recommendation? You can follow it but you don't have to. A recommendation isn't a verdict.

I wanted to know the truth. I didn't want to resign myself. Maybe I had been lucky. Yes, me. Maybe? Maybe. No. You're not to use "maybe"—that horrible word has fooled you for too long. I forbid you even to think it.

We didn't fall asleep until the early morning hours. It was almost noon when we got up. The sun was shining. There were no fresh rolls, but there was lots of coffee in the blue pot, and it seemed to me as though even the bushes in the garden were embracing.

I was home again. The house, the familiar landscape, being together with Ralph, enthralled me, so that the last few months seemed ever more unreal. If I could not feel, could not grasp, all those things that had happened in Kiev, how much less could I comprehend them afterward, now that I was so very far away from there in space and time, as well as emotionally. And I was doing well. I was feeling well. That incident after my arrival? Just a sudden weak spell. Readjustment. Nothing more.

I never again met any of my fellow students. They had come from many different regions and, after leaving Kiev, each returned to his or her own hometown. We didn't see one another, didn't even think of one another, never exchanged stories about our experiences.

Perhaps we could have taken some joint action. But how? And what? There was nothing we could have done retroactively. And our chances of accomplishing anything were really so distressingly small. Besides, like me, each of them was secretly hoping: I'm sure I was lucky. I'm sure of it.

Only rarely did I think of Laura. It was getting harder to remember her clearly. When I tried, only a vague picture came to mind. Sometimes I would hear her say a few words, would see a quick gesture, a vigorous shake of the head. I wanted to answer her letters but didn't know what to say. Mostly I had no time, or when I had the time I didn't feel like it.

And what could I have written to her? That I'd finally had some luck? How I was getting on with Ralph? That those last months in Kiev seemed to me like an absurd nightmare? So I postponed writing from one week to the next.

It's unpleasant to receive letters from someone who reminds you of things you'd rather forget. You don't open the letters right away. They get misplaced, then they disappear. Sometime or other they turn up again, but, by then, it's too late to reply. In the end, you burn them.

To keep faith with my mad delusion, I betrayed Laura. The years spent in Kiev, especially the last three months, were not—must not be—more than a nightmare from which I had fortunately awakened. How easy this betrayal was. But isn't betrayal always easy when it coincides with your own desires?

There would have been plenty of opportunities to connect with reality. But I didn't want to. I didn't listen to any news reports about the disaster. Somehow I always managed to have something else to do just then. By sheer coincidence.

I remember only one radio program: It was called "Listeners Ask, the Experts Answer." A housewife called up and asked whether she could eat food she had canned, and where and how she could have it tested for radioactivity.

I shook my head in disbelief. Put my hands over my ears. Then I began to laugh hysterically until tears came to my eyes. Could it be that people in the GDR, 750 miles away from the site, were having their home-canned food tested? Foolish woman!

Later, I heard that same laughter in my dreams. Others were now laughing at *me* just as hysterically and brutally.

The way Father was suddenly getting along with Ralph should have made me suspicious; he didn't raise any objections to Ralph's staying the night and sleeping with me. I should have wondered why it didn't bother anyone when I turned the volume of the music way up, why Mother did all the chores I used to do around the house. But I ignored all these little signs. I didn't see it, this grand entente of understanding and indulgence. Everything seemed to be all right.

Oh, come on. Don't kid yourself. It wasn't long before you

started up out of a dream one night, bathed in sweat. Relieved to find it was only a dream, albeit a terrifying one.

You got up, put on your bathrobe, lit a cigarette, went over to the window, and looked out into the garden. It was your first nightmare since you'd come back, and it showed you what was wrong.

I am a woman made of glass. I stand, immobile and transparent, in one of the classrooms at my old school, but there are no children sitting at the desks; rather, they are university students. A gray-bearded, balding old man wearing a white lab coat stands beside me at the front of the room. Using a pointer he indicates various parts of my body and identifies them in a foreign language.

Why doesn't he use Latin, I wonder. He is hurting me with his pointed stick. I tell him to stop jabbing me. But he refuses to be distracted and pretends he hasn't heard me, even though I spoke in a loud, clear voice. Finally, he puts the pointer down. He comes up to me and removes individual parts of my body: first a hand, then an arm, then a breast. He explains something to the students I cannot understand. When he shows them my breast, their faces become serious, and they stare. The professor leaves the room without reattaching my missing body parts.

The students jump up as though they'd been waiting for this moment. They drape a scarf around me and put a silly-looking cap on my head. They spitefully reposition the various parts of my body, twist my arms and legs until I look like a cripple. Finally, they glue a black beard on my face.

Facial hair growth in women. Hormone treatment for cancer. I knew very well what the dream meant. And this desperate attempt to defend myself even though I couldn't move. It was all as clear and obvious as if it were in a picture book. That's just the point; it wasn't *only a recommendation.*

Then I was standing at the window, afraid to go back to bed and surrender to my subconscious, over which I had no control and which did not want to play along with my delusion of carefree happiness. At some point, too tired to keep my eyes open, I fell asleep in a chair. The next morning I woke up with a crick in my neck and tried to ignore the dream.

Everything would turn out all right. Everything really *was* all right. Why tarnish these beautiful days with Ralph by talking about stupid dreams? The time would come soon enough when I would have to go to work, and Ralph to the university, and the daily routine, with its demands and problems, would take hold of us. So don't spoil these few days that were free of dissension.

Always this need for peace and harmony, maneuvering myself from one self-deception to the next. Up to the very end. Almost.

|

Actually, I felt tired and worn-out right from my first day at work. I blamed it on having to get up so early every day. I was already exhausted by the time I arrived at work after standing on the crowded, early morning commuter train. Then in the plant, tentatively establishing a wary relationship with my fellow workers; the noise of the machines in the huge workrooms; the fluorescent lights; and the dry, stifling air. Wasn't that enough to make you tired? No chance to sit down and rest, aside from the short scheduled breaks. No chance to take a longer break for an hour or so as we had done at the university. The eight and three-quarter hours at work seemed an eternity.

How they kept their eyes on the newcomer. The sewing-machine operators wanted to trip me up; the supervisors tried to find out what problems I might cause them. I had the feeling that each was looking for some weak spot in me, just waiting for me to make my first mistake. I counted the minutes till the workday was over.

In the evening I took the crowded train home. At last, in my room, dog tired, I would sit around, smoke, or put things away, totally unable to concentrate on reading a book; or I'd lie down to sleep for an hour. But often I didn't wake up till ten or eleven o'clock at night. Then I would undress and go to bed to sleep some more. I was quite unable to cope but didn't want to admit it. And as long as I somehow made it through the day, no one cared.

In September I became ill for the first time. At work. Feeling as though I might throw up any minute, I kept running to the lavatory. I held my wrists under the cold-water faucet, washed my face, and, with much effort, just barely made it to quitting time. No one cared. After all, it was my problem. I thought so, too. It was my problem. My own personal problem.

When was it that the head of the personnel department called me in? It was right at the beginning, after only a couple of days on the job. No questions about what had happened in Kiev, or how I felt. Rather a speech, a lecture: They didn't want to have any trouble in the plant; they had enough problems already, and they didn't want to be burdened with more. I wasn't to talk about the city where I had studied. And when I went to see the manager, he said the same thing.

It all seemed so unnecessary. These warnings, these admonitions. I wasn't interested in talking about anything concerning my time in Kiev. To me, that wasn't merely months ago; it seemed like years, decades ago. Even if people had asked me about it, what could I have told them?

I wouldn't have been able to explain the situation in a comprehensible way: our behavior, the way we dealt with the risks. How we only gradually got a picture of what had happened, our uncertainty in assessing the problem, how helpless and disheartened we felt about not being able to do or change anything, and our perpetual hope: It can't possibly be that terrible—I'm sure I'll be spared.

"Good God! You were much too close. Why didn't you get out of there?" That's easy to say, afterward.

Now I know: The head of personnel and the plant manager were afraid that I would talk about the official lies, the stalling, how we had been treated like incompetents.

But that fall I wanted to be left alone in my deceptive state of peace and quiet; I didn't want to talk at all. Of my own accord I did whatever was necessary to conceal what had happened: I was silent. It was only the manner in which I had been forbidden to speak that incited me, challenged me to break my silence, to step over the line at least once.

That's why I agreed to meet with the writer even though I didn't know him; why I didn't refuse to see him when he telephoned in September.

What is it that makes you want to talk—to one human being, at least—about things that should not be discussed? What do you get out of it, other than the mistaken notion that the other person will help you cope with your problems? And you know very well that's just a fantasy. You are and always will be alone with your fate. Talking doesn't affect anything except the moment when you are talking, when you might have been doing something else— smoking a cigarette, having a drink, watching a film, whatever.

And what are the other person's motives for listening to you? Why does he join you in perpetuating your fantasy? For minutes or hours at a time? Self-interest. Perhaps he's just lonely; perhaps it's his profession; or he wants to write about it; or something like that.

Did I want to talk to him then, or didn't I? There's this inner turmoil, this confused back and forth. To talk. Not to talk. Yes, talk. A little. Make a start. In violation of the prohibition. "I won't let them tell me what not to do!" When actually I had forbidden myself to talk about it. And not just to talk, but even to think about it.

I still see him coming toward me, smiling, his eyes attentive. He told me his name and held out his hand. I extended mine. He took it in a moderately firm grasp but held it a moment longer than I would have preferred.

Then, neither of us saying a word, we walked up the street side by side, looking for a café. What devil drove me to agree to meet him? Suddenly I wished I were standing in the crowded commuter train, surrounded by silent people who didn't know me and wouldn't talk to me; suddenly I wished I were at home, in my own room, a blanket over my head, my eyes closed. Anything, just so I wouldn't have to go on walking next to this man who knew that I had been in Kiev, who wanted to know more, and who would soon be plying me with questions.

Utter muddleheaded orneriness. Because they had forbidden

me to talk, I had agreed to meet him, even though I didn't want to. And instead of telling him that I had changed my mind, that I didn't feel like talking about these things, I went along and played this game of hide-and-seek. "I don't know whether I can be of any help to you." Blah . . . blah. And he tried very hard. Held the door open for me, helped me out of my coat, looked for an isolated table in a corner trying to create the right "atmosphere." I hid behind the menu and ordered coffee and a dish of ice cream.

I still remember the first thing I said in this fateful conversation. "I don't have much time—left," I said. I wanted to set a time limit for the interview. Wanted to get away as quickly as possible. But the little word "left" had sneaked into the sentence.

I don't have much time—left. Crazy. As though I had already known then. Known beforehand.

He wanted to write something about the accident, its aftermath, and I was afraid. What if he were to publish his piece in the West? If they found out that I had spoken with him, what sort of consequences could that have? Just because *he* was taking chances, why should I let myself be drawn in?

There it was again. That greatest fear. The fear of unforeseeable consequences if I didn't behave as expected.

But that's not all. Damn it. Don't deceive yourself. Not now. Not here. You were also afraid of your memories, of your suppressed feelings, your own black hole of despair. *Only a recommendation . . .*

He sensed my resistance. Assured me of confidentiality. Said in his piece he'd change the names of people and circumstances to make it impossible for anyone to identify me. So tenacious.

And I resisted. "I don't know whether I could tell you anything that would be of interest to you. After all, everything is more or less well known."

He didn't let up. "What were you thinking at the time? How did you react? How did you explain your great need for sleep? What did you want to do? What did you do? Why did you do what you did? What did you think afterward? A day later? A month later?"

Suddenly I saw everything that happened in Kiev clearly before my eyes, more clearly than when I was in the midst of it all. I talked and talked, as though I were talking to myself. The questions he asked seemed so natural.

His manner, a mixture of intensity and reserve, prompted me to keep talking against my will. I even spoke about my moods and emotions, something I normally would have kept to myself. At some point I abruptly became aware of this. I stopped speaking, breaking off the conversation in midsentence. I was terrified.

|

Should I have talked to him again after that? Up to that point the conversation had done me good. But I hadn't ventured into the more thorny aspects. The talk with the doctor, for example. Who knows what would have happened then, what would have surfaced from within me?

Would anything have been changed by such conversations? Certainly not in my situation. Would I have learned to deal with my problems more openly? More confidently? With greater self-assurance? Would I have integrated my experiences, my memories, instead of suppressing them? *Only a recommendation . . .*

Could be. I don't know. Could also be that I might have come to the obvious conclusion sooner. It's futile now to think about it all again.

This conversation was different from those I'd had with my parents or with Ralph. They tried to spare me, and so they confined me to playing just one role. That of the sick person, the incurably sick person. A leper. The writer, on the other hand, didn't try to spare me. On the contrary, he tackled me head-on. At least he tried. And I tried to block him.

In spite of that, I felt as though the wall between my reason and my emotions was beginning to crumble. I came close to losing my self-control. Close to breaking down and crying. In front of him. A stranger.

And what if his project had worked out? What did I have to lose by speaking to him? What did I risk? I ask that now. After the fact. But at the time I was glad that I had terminated the conversation, angry I had gone even this far.

I had finished my ice cream some time ago. The coffee in the cup had gotten cold. How long he looked at me when we were done. My face, hair, shoulders, breasts, hands. As if he wanted to remember how I looked. But maybe I just imagined it. Anyway, he took a deep breath and gently shook his head as though he wanted to chase away an unwelcome thought. Well, yes. But nothing more than that.

He needn't have given me his address. He knew very well that I wouldn't get in touch with him. Terror-struck, I had stopped talking to him, and after that there was nothing for me to reconsider.

He really needn't have called me again at work. Needn't have written that letter. "Think of the responsibility you have . . . , the problems of nuclear energy must not be suppressed and minimized . . . Think of those who are suffering from radiation sickness, those who have silently died of it . . . You experienced things that still lie ahead for the rest of us. Please share your concerns with me . . ."

Such hype, I thought. I simply didn't want to. Why me of all people? There were plenty of others. Let him ask them. After all, I wasn't the only one. Such exaggeration: "You experienced things that still lie ahead for the rest of us."

He's imagining the worst-case scenario, I thought. What grandiose ideas he has. As though his story—even if I had gone on talking to him, even if he had written it all down, even if they had published it—could have changed anything, reversed it, even delayed it.

▌

I met him too soon. Some months later I would have talked. After my stay in the hospital. And now I'm talking to this pastor, to make up for the conversations that didn't take place then.

Still, at the time I didn't immediately throw away his letter or his address. But a few weeks later I burned both. Out of fear.

Come on! This doesn't make sense. Don't keep tormenting yourself! Don't belittle yourself again. He, too, was afraid.

What would have happened had I had a clear and unequivocal understanding of my own situation several months earlier? What if, triggered by his questions, my illusion of security had collapsed? Would he have set off something in me for which he would have borne some responsibility? Would I have had a nervous breakdown? Fits of rage or crying jags? Perhaps gone mad? Maybe I would have done then, last fall, what I only now have the strength to do. And he would have been the causal agent. My destiny would have become intertwined with his. He ought to be glad that I bravely chose to remain silent.

When we met, the entire problem was just an interesting topic for him to write about. He wasn't touched by it. This might have changed as he got more involved with "my case." Then he might have had nightmares, might have had to reach for his sleeping pills. No, it wasn't entirely my fault that our conversation had not continued.

There was also something in his manner that acted as an obstacle to further conversations. Something in his tone of voice. Something warily defensive in his body language. That slightly shocked look in his eyes as I spoke. The deep breaths he took when we parted at the train station. When my train finally got under way. The exaggerated tone of his letter. Trivial things. Perhaps.

He had tried everything, and it didn't work. I balked. He was excused. Now he couldn't and didn't have to continue. Not with me, not on this subject. After that, I never heard from him again.

|

What's the sense in all this? Why keep thinking about it? Is it only because I'll be talking with the pastor again tomorrow? Making excuses for myself. I wanted to remain silent. Now I'm talking and I need to justify myself. I was finished with all this, and now I'm beginning again. It all starts with talking. Weighing one's words, remembering, anticipating. Arriving at a mutual understanding. The spoken sentences, like hawsers, tie me to the supposed realities. And draw me further and further into the past. Only by keeping silent can there be total separation. But I won't come to any more understandings; I don't want any phony understandings. This pastor wants to drag me over the line. Over to his side. First into no-man's-land, and then to his side. Division of labor: The doctors keep me here physically. They know their efforts are futile. They can't constantly keep watch over me. One of these days I'll leave this hospital. The pastor knows very well that I'm still on the other side.

I'm tired. I ought to sleep now. Close your eyes. Stop staring at the streetlight. Don't listen to the nurse's footsteps anymore.

Perhaps I might have answered his letter later. Somewhat later. After all, I had his address. In any case, a few weeks later.

It's pointless. I don't want to. Still. Look here. At least don't act like a coward now. Not now, not in your own eyes.

I had allowed myself to be intimidated. By this dapper Stasi* monkey who was waiting for me in the personnel office. By him.

"I'm from the union, and I'd like to talk with you. Just the two of us over a cup of coffee and a cigarette. Oh, excuse me. Do you smoke?"

So casual. And along with that a searching look that made me feel naked.

"How do you like working in the plant?"

"It's not bad, but then I haven't been here very long." I think: What business is that of yours?

"Have you settled into the new job?"

"I have to get to know the various departments first before I can give you a proper assessment."

---

* Stasi was the East German State Security Service. Its agents and informers infiltrated all spheres of German Democratic Republic society. —TRANS.

You in that suit, with your manicured fingernails, I'm sure you haven't done a bit of real work so far today. And me, sitting here in this blue smock.

"How are you getting along with your male co-workers?"

"Oh well, that varies, as you might expect."

What does he mean, "male co-workers"? Almost all the people working here are women. Why does he have that stupid grin on his face all the time?

"I can understand your reticence. After all, you don't know me. But this can be an advantage, too. If you were to confide in someone working in the factory, she might tell someone else and that person might tell another until pretty soon it's made the rounds. That would be unpleasant. Yet, everybody needs to talk to someone about their worries and problems. And that's precisely why I came to see you."

"I have no problems, and I don't know what I could talk to you about."

You can keep blabbing on about confidentiality, about how it won't go any further, and so on. But it won't work with me.

"No, no. I don't want to talk you into seeing difficulties where they don't exist. But, just between you and me, I know which university you attended and when. Surely that couldn't have been an easy situation for you. Perhaps you have certain things on your mind stemming from that. Isn't it better to talk to someone like me who has a receptive ear, whose job it is to concern himself with the well-being of other people, rather than, perhaps in desperation, to talk to people who may have dubious motives and only want to exploit you. Once such people get what they're after, they disappear and you're left alone with your problems. They'll forget you."

"I don't know what you're talking about."

Does he know something? Or is he just bluffing? Had one of the women in the plant talked? Who? Was the phone bugged? Or maybe he doesn't know anything and is only acting as if he did. To intimidate me. "Everybody needs to talk to someone . . ." Otherwise he would be more specific: He'd say, "We know that . . ."

"Look, we have the means and connections to help you and to stand by you. For instance, how about a four- or six-week health cure? Or something like that. Think it over."

"Thanks for the offer. I'll consider it."

He must be off his rocker. This guy. What does he really want?

"Very well. In addition, I also want to warn you not to let yourself be exploited by other people for any dubious projects. You don't need that sort of thing. I don't have any doubts about your political views, your personal honesty. But one can never know what effects certain opinions or words dropped in casual conversation can have—could have—in a different context."

"I do my work to the best of my ability, and I'm not interested in having conversations about things that are over and done with."

I'd like to know what he knows and what he doesn't know. What a relief it will be to get out of here.

"Well, so much the better. It's always a good thing to be able to distinguish the important things from the unimportant, to see the larger picture, and to be able to generalize from one's personal situation. By the way, what do you do after work?"

"There's not much time left after work. I have a long commute. Sometimes I go dancing, sometimes I take a walk. Nothing special."

Some nerve, to get personal now. If I met you outside the plant, I'd send you packing in no time.

"Think about our conversation on one of your walks. And if you have something on your mind, you can call me anytime. Here's my telephone number."

"Thank you. Well, I'll get back to work now."

He didn't even get the innuendo. Offered me his smooth, cold hand.

|

I shudder even now when I think of it. With a lump in my throat, I walked out through the office of the head of personnel, into the hall, and to the lunchroom to have a cigarette. Always this fear. What do they know? What do they want from me? And why? The lump in my throat wouldn't go away.

Why did I put up with this? I wasn't about to call him; that was for sure. Throw away his telephone number? Of course. But why didn't I lodge a complaint about this outrage, this summons? Even if a protest wouldn't have done any good. Why hadn't I simply refused to meet with him in the first place?

I talked myself into believing that conversations like this wouldn't influence me. That I would be just as I had been before. But I did throw away the writer's letter, either that very evening or the next. Out of fear. Don't keep anything incriminating. Not at home either. You never know, a stupid coincidence or something like that.

I allowed them to intimidate me.

But to myself I rationalized. "I want to be left in peace. No conversations with anyone. Not interested in talking about what happened to me. Quite inconsistent to keep the letter. What for?"

So tear it up. Burn it. And why didn't I just crumple it up and throw it away? I was afraid. That was the stupidest part of it. Not afraid of the particles that kept emitting their radiation in secret places somewhere in my body, but vaguely afraid of conversations, of suggestions, of dreams that made me remember. I didn't feel endangered by what really threatened my health, my life, but by some anonymous unassailable power that remained incomprehensible, unfathomable, and against which I felt defenseless. Against which no struggle, no defense, was possible.

And then Father asked me who had sent the letter. My father who ordinarily showed no interest whatsoever in my mail.

I told him about the writer, that we had met and talked. Quite routinely. And suddenly Father jumped up, stared at me, and shouted: "What does he want from you? Why is he asking you questions? Mother and I are glad that you've finally come home. That you can enjoy your plants, your room. That things are working out between you and Ralph. Why churn up everything when the wound has just begun to heal, is beginning to mend? Who knows what you'll be drawn into through your contact with him? And you'll draw us into it, too." He continued in a calmer voice, "Try to understand that we want you to get well; we want you to be able to forget this whole thing and live happily in this house."

"Father," I said, getting up and walking over to him, "I wasn't going to see him again anyway." And he put his arms around me and held me close. I savored this embrace, consented to the silence for which we each had our own motives. But at my back, I sensed a yawning abyss . . .

Had this author come along several months later, I would have talked to him. Without listening to Father. Or to that union guy. Without giving in to my fear, my tiredness. But in those days. No. In those days, I remained silent.

I can empathize with all those who are silent and keep hoping, hoping, and say nothing. Only when it's too late do they speak up to defend themselves. If at all. Unless, like me, they secretly clear out. As I intended to. Would have. Should have. But didn't.

|

It was the end of September. I didn't get my period. Found myself staring at the oddest things, sometimes for minutes at a time, my mind a blank. When someone spoke to me, I would surface from another world, look around, and, for several seconds, I would have no idea where I was, what they wanted of me.

Still, I didn't think much about it. No. In Kiev, after the accident, I had missed periods, too. And I wasn't pregnant then either.

And now? In the mornings I was mildly surprised when the alarm clock went off, when I awoke and immediately realized: another day. I felt a quiet satisfaction. So there. Something's happening in my body. But it doesn't necessarily mean anything. No grounds for joy, no reason to be troubled. Not for a long time yet.

It was really mean of me not to tell Ralph.

I knew that he didn't want a child. Not while he was still in school. Not before we had our own apartment. Maybe in a few years. After all, we had just recently revived our relationship. Had to get to know each other again after the long separation . . . All that was true. But not for me.

What should I have done? *Only a recommendation . . .*
Should I have told him how much I wanted a child? *Only a
recommendation . . .* After all, I had even concealed that wish
from myself. I didn't weigh the pros and cons. *Only a recommendation . . .* No. I had the vague feeling that it was important
for me now to have a small living being. Now. Not sometime in
the future.

And I wanted to make it happen. To get rid of all the fuss that
enveloped me like a spiderweb. To prove to myself and to all the
others: "Look at me! I'm healthy. I have a healthy child. I'm a
happy young mother. I'm not a leper, not a sick woman who has
to be treated with special care. I don't want to be coddled; I don't
want others to tell me what I can and can't talk about. There's
nothing more to be said. I'm not a guinea pig, not a literary
subject. I'm a normal woman with a completely normal baby."

The children. By that time I was already pregnant. Was that
the beginning of October? For three or four days in a row there
had been another spell of very warm weather. I remember it well:
a sunny day, and I had looked longingly out the window. In the
afternoon I took a bus downtown to go shopping. By now, blue-
black clouds were gathering and settling over the city like a dark
blanket. I went into a department store to wait out the rain. It
was terribly crowded in the aisles and at the counters. The heat
had built up, and, with perspiring people all around me, it became unbearable. Also, I was overdressed. The ventilation system
made futile attempts to circulate the heavy, stuffy air. I wanted to
get out. Better not to buy anything and get wet in the rain than
suffocate in this stale, oppressive air that smelled of sweat, plas-
tics, and solvents. In front of the exit the crowds were even denser.
Most people, expecting a thunderstorm to break at any moment,
stayed in the lobby. There was a constant stream of people coming in, fleeing the storm. Nevertheless, I walked toward this clus-
ter of humanity intending to push my way through. I didn't care
about those who were standing there; they were just a collection

of bodies that were in my way. Driven by the intolerable smell, the heat, and the desire to finally get out into the open, I kept pushing forward. But then I literally got wedged between other people's bodies. No way to move forward or backward, and the crowding kept getting worse. I felt I would be crushed or suffocated, so I struggled on and was able to push past several more people when a deep, gruff voice said:

"Can't you see that you can't go any farther? Don't be so inconsiderate. There are children standing here!"

Only then did I look at the people around me, at the indignant face of a bearded man directly in front of me, and next to him and behind him quite a few children. I stopped, stammered an excuse.

These children. Some with twisted, squinty eyes; over there a face contorted in a grimace. One child looked as though he were in terrible pain. And yet, he seemed to be enjoying himself. It's just that he had no other way to express his joy than to twist his face like this, to open his mouth crookedly, and to squeeze his eyes shut. Saliva was dribbling from one corner of his mouth onto his parka, which was already quite damp.

The crowd from behind pushed me deeper into the ranks of the children. I felt twisted, spastic arms reaching for me, for my child. Suddenly I knew for certain that I was pregnant. I was seized by indescribable panic. I thought my head was splitting, my skull about to shatter. I couldn't stand the sight of these horribly deformed children one minute longer. Something in me rebelled. Trembling, I covered my eyes with my hands and heard myself groaning loudly. Without thinking, I ran forward, pushing aside whatever was in my way.

I ran and ran, contorted mouths smiling at me, spastic arms holding me back, wild looks pursuing me.

Two blocks away I stopped, soaked with perspiration from running so fast. Not really breathing; only groaning. My heart was pounding so hard I thought my chest would explode. The terrible department store was now no longer in view. I thought I would die of thirst.

I could ring for the nurse and say, "I just woke up and I'd like something to drink." That would be understandable in this heat. But no, I don't want anything for myself anymore. Nothing. I won't ask for anything anymore.

That day I went into a café. At the counter I asked for a glass of water, unable to wait another minute. I drank it in greedy gulps, wordlessly set the glass down, and left. The woman behind the counter looked after me with concern.

The rain wouldn't come. Exhausted, I sat down on a bench, still shaking. Convulsive sobs forced their way up through my throat, which felt as though someone were trying to choke me. Something was forcing its way to the surface, something I had till then wanted to suppress. *Only a recommendation . . .* perhaps it was a verdict after all. The children. That shouldn't be allowed. Anything, anything, just not to give birth to a disabled child. Having to look at it every day, one's entire lifetime. It would be like a mirror, showing you that something had happened to you that you never wanted to admit.

As if drugged or in a trance I took the bus home, went to the bathroom, opened the medicine cabinet, grabbed the pills. I pressed one of the tablets through the foil, put it on my tongue, and swallowed it with some water. Only then did I go upstairs to my room; I undressed, lay down on the bed, and fell asleep.

From that day on, I couldn't sleep nights without taking those pills. First one, then two, then three. When I awoke in the morning I had dreadful headaches; my arms and legs felt as heavy as lead. It required a great effort to get up, to take my first steps, to get dressed, to eat. Each day, pure torment.

I felt sorry for you, Ralph. Really. When you came to see me in the evening, I would be tired, all in, and cool toward you. I didn't feel like going out or doing anything. I was barely able to listen to the stories you told about the university, your seminars, the lectures you attended. I saw your mouth opening and closing, but I didn't hear the words. I sat there as though watching a silent film. A continuous parallel stream of words reeled off within me, a completely different discourse having nothing to do with what you were saying, that kept me from listening to you and from speaking.

But I want to be pregnant. I want to have a healthy child. A child. Not a cripple. I am going to prove to myself and to you that I can have healthy children. That I'm all right. Healthy. Capable. I don't need your *recommendations* . . .

My thoughts kept circling around this same theme in ever different variations. But this was precisely what I couldn't talk to you about, Ralph. No wonder you became less and less interested in spending time with me. I must have been dull company since I didn't seem to be interested in anything and just sat there, silent and apathetic, no matter what you talked about.

‖

Let there never again be a time like that. Such days. Such nights. I gave birth to monsters. Clumps of flesh without recognizable limbs. Pulled out of my body with glowing tongs. Scaly creatures grew within me, grew and grew until I burst. I gave birth to cephalopods who lacked torsos, their shapeless limbs growing out of their heads.

‖

The nights you slept with me became increasingly rare. You didn't come to see me for days at a time. You seldom asked how I felt. Whenever I woke up at night with a cry of horror, bathed in sweat, you'd want to know, "Are you feeling all right?"

"Just a bad dream," I would say, and by then you were usually asleep again. And I entwined my arms and legs about you like a clinging vine.

My fear of falling asleep increased daily, and yet I yearned to sleep a long, quiet, dreamless sleep from which I would awake refreshed and happy.

In early November, when I threw up for the first time, I wasn't quite sure what caused it. Did it have something to do with my suspected yet still unconfirmed pregnancy? Was it a consequence of my daily use of sedatives, sleeping pills? Or was it because I was overtired from many sleepless nights? Perhaps it was related to my irregular eating. It wouldn't be surprising if, for these reasons alone, my body was reacting like this.

I wanted never again to have to stagger down the stairs, pressing my hand to my mouth. I couldn't hold it in. The vomit ran through my fingers, dribbled, spurted onto the carpet, the plants, the banister. The distance to the bathroom seemed endless. I bent over the toilet, retching. On and on. My stomach, my entire body, gripped by wave after wave of cramps.

Mother came out of her room and, with worry in her voice, asked, "What's the matter? My God, what's wrong?"

"Nothing, nothing, it's all right. I think there was something wrong with the food in the plant cafeteria yesterday. I already felt ill in the afternoon. But now it's over. Don't worry, it's better already."

You stood there in your nightgown, your hair all tousled, and you shook your head in disbelief.

"I'm sorry," I said.

Without speaking, you stroked my hair and sent me back to bed. You took a pail and a rag and wiped up what there was to wipe. After that, I always took a bowl to my room in the evening.

It had turned cold. The end of November. There was hoarfrost on the streets, and even though I was already wearing my winter coat I felt chilled all the time. Still, I was feeling better. It had been several days since I had to throw up. On the train to work in the mornings, people no longer offered me their seats as they had when they saw my chalk-white face, fearing I would topple over any minute.

What was I thinking that morning? I can't remember. The train was heated. Someone I had seen several times before nodded to me briefly. A few days before, I had started working in a new department at the plant. I felt well, my co-workers accepted me, talked to me about their marriages, joked around, didn't ask me any questions.

That day the weather was stormy. I recall that in detail. The wind tore at the bare trees, snapped off branches, and blew solitary leaves along the streets. Where did they come from so late in the year?

I sat by the window in the plant's lunchroom. Words were flying back and forth like tennis balls. Half-empty coffee cups stood on the table. Several women were reading newspapers; others discussed the previous evening's television programs. One woman talked about her husband who had again come home drunk and had beaten her. She wanted to get a divorce but didn't dare go to court because she was afraid he would become even more violent. A co-worker told her: "If things don't get better, you and your kids can move in with me for a while."

I looked out the window. Several of the women began to stack empty cups. They folded up their newspapers. I was about to get up, too, when suddenly I felt a stabbing pain in my lower abdomen. A cramp knotted my insides. I couldn't stand up straight. Pressed my hands to my belly.

Walking stiffly, like a marionette, I tried to get to the door. My hand missed the door knob, reached into nothingness, and I plunged down a bottomless void.

When I came to, I felt something damp, warm, and sticky between my legs. I attempted to raise my head, trying to see what was going on around me, why I was lying on the lunchroom floor surrounded by co-workers who looked like giants, with incredibly long bodies and tiny heads. More blood flowed out of me.

"Don't move," someone in a white lab coat said. "Please be sensible."

Then they put me on a stretcher and carried me through the hallway of the plant. I closed my eyes. Like a child who doesn't want to be seen but hasn't yet realized that others can still see her even when she closes her eyes.

Now they all know, I thought. Then I was pushed into an ambulance and brought to the hospital. Scraped out. Out of the cave in my belly in which no child wanted to nest. Bloody scraps of flesh were torn out of this grave, just as I had foreseen in my dreams.

I felt paralyzed. This proved it. Something wasn't quite right with me. What I had only vaguely suspected up to then, the thing that kept happening to me in my dreams, the thing I didn't want to admit, no longer could be denied. *Only a recommendation . . . Only a recommendation . . . Only a recommendation . . .* The words of the doctor in Kiev went round and round in my head.

No, *not* merely a recommendation, Doctor, a verdict, a sentence.

After the accident, most of the women in Kiev had had abortions. I knew that. Half a year isn't ten years. Ten years could also turn into twenty. Or no years at all. A recommendation is not only a recommendation . . . the words kept going through my mind as I rode up and down in noiseless elevators, was pushed along white hallways and into white sickrooms.

You have been marked "infertile and sick" because you were there, because you got too high a dose. Because you didn't draw the obvious conclusions, didn't take the appropriate steps, didn't clear out. You didn't want to understand, and now you've got your bloody penalty.

And then words were said in that hospital that were supposed to cheer me up. To comfort me. But they sounded like mockery to me.

"It will get better . . . after all you're still young . . . This happens quite frequently. No reason to panic . . . with your constitution . . . You'll have many children."

"You don't have to tell me fairy tales," I told them. "I was in Kiev in the spring and in the summer. I didn't know then what was going on, but now I know. And now I won't let anyone put anything over on me anymore. Not anyone."

That's what I said. There was silence then. No one spoke. They left me and went to another room. The only reaction came from a young doctor: "What a thing to say! There doesn't have to be a connection. Why not wait awhile and not get all worked up for nothing. In any case, getting upset is not good for you. You must rest to regain your strength. Then everything will look different."

No, this time I didn't let them fool me. I had counted on this child. Had waited, and hoped for a judgment that would set me free, the dismissal of false charges lodged against me. This child was going to free me from self-doubts, from the uncertainty bred by a *recommendation*. And now the recommendation had turned into a verdict. I could no longer dismiss this miscarriage as a slight mishap that could happen to anyone.

And that's not all.

Suddenly I saw the constant fatigue, the vomiting, the malaise in a totally different context. These weren't merely my body's reactions to the pills I had taken, not merely symptoms of pregnancy. Rather, they were the harbingers of the illness that afflicted me.

Suddenly everything appeared in a different light. I felt as though someone had thrown a net over me. I was entangled, and now an invisible hand was slowly but steadily drawing the net tighter. I would have to adjust to getting along in an increasingly confined space.

As was the case in Kiev, I didn't feel like getting up. I just wanted to sleep and sleep, hoping not to wake up the next morning. Illusory hope. It required a decision, an act, for me not to wake up anymore. Otherwise, this messed-up life of mine would go on and on until it couldn't go on anymore. Until it stopped on its own.

How short-lived are insights. How easily the mind allows

itself to be bribed by good regular meals, a moderate amount of rest, and a preoccupation with the rituals of daily life. Physically, I was feeling better. I was able to get up, walk about in the hospital hallways. Often I stood at the window looking out at the bare trees and the leaves decomposing in the street and in the courtyard.

Each tree has a new beginning. In the spring. When the days get longer, the sun's rays fall more perpendicularly on the earth, and the tree puts forth new leaves. Why shouldn't I also have a new beginning? Foolish thoughts, quickly overtaken by reality. But I had such thoughts then.

On the next-to-last day of my hospital stay I went to see the ward doctor. I don't remember why. The door to his office was open. No one was inside. I was about to leave when I noticed several files on his desk. Hesitantly I inched closer, wondering whether it wouldn't be better to wait for him outside in the hall. Quite without thinking, I read some of the names on the files. I had already taken a few steps toward the door when I realized that *my* name was on one of those folders.

Should I have left the room? Perhaps. But I wanted to know more. So I went back and randomly leafed through the assortment of papers and graphs in my file.

Discharged on . . . The patient . . . Hurriedly I began to read: "It cannot be entirely ruled out that there is a connection between the dose of radiation the patient received and her miscarriage. However, given the numerous other possible factors that might have led to the miscarriage, there is no compelling reason to assume that this was the cause. The patient says that for some time she has been suffering from insomnia and nervous vomiting. Her general condition is satisfactory and improving. In principle, there can be no objection on our part to future pregnancies."

In principle, there can be no objection . . . Quite a lot of objections, Doctor. Quite a lot.

I still remember repeating the words to myself, "No compelling reason to assume . . . cannot be entirely ruled out . . . no compelling reason to assume . . . cannot be entirely ruled out . . ."

The phrases whirled round and round in my head like a carousel. I dropped the file and left the office.

|

Kafkaesque. The trial is under way now. You are charged. You don't know with what. You are judged and sentenced. To infertility, to death. You don't know when the sentence will be carried out . . . But heaven help you if you anticipate the verdict. Then you'll be guarded like a convicted felon. In rooms with sealed windows. In rooms without mirrors. No knife at mealtimes. No handles on the ward doors leading outside.

|

The next morning the hospital's chief of medicine was making his rounds accompanied by a flock of men and women in white lab coats. He came to my bed, listened to a summary of my case by one of the other doctors, and looked cursorily at my chart without really reading it. Then he nodded at me and said, "So far, your test results are all right. We can discharge you today. Take good care." With that he was about to move on.

I gathered all my courage. What little I had left. After all, this was about *me,* damn it. At first, my voice cracked. I thought: Don't let them push you aside, just keep talking. "You want to discharge me today," I said. "But I want to know what's going on in my body. I want to know whether I can still have children. How big the risk is. I want to know exactly how much radiation I got. And once and for all, I want to know whether a recommendation is a recommendation or whether it is a verdict."

"You mustn't exaggerate the situation," he said. "Although, theoretically, radiation can affect the genetic material, the relatively small dose of radiation you received at such considerable distance from the site of the accident can in no way be related to your miscarriage. There are too many factors to be considered for us to be able to give you a definite prognosis. It is possible that with your next pregnancy you would have no problems whatsoever. On the other hand, it could be that some problems might come to light in your grandchildren or great-grandchildren. There is a great deal of conjecture about all this. Connections cannot be conclusively proven. So far, there hasn't been enough research done on the effects of radioactive fallout on the human organism."

He wanted to comfort me, to "enlighten" me. Wanted to answer his patient's questions correctly. *Connections cannot be conclusively proven . . . So far, there hasn't been enough research done* . . . I said nothing. I had the feeling I was grappling with a cloud. It was all so friendly, so meaningless, so futile.

As if dangers are real only once they have been proven beyond a doubt. As though up to then I had been protected from all dangers and could imagine myself safe. My life is ruined, even without your research! It has been spoiled even without any of your test results!

When there has been interference with nature and all sorts of poisons and radioactive material have been released into the atmosphere, why don't you—in judging the dangers—proceed from the worst-case scenario? If you're going to gird yourself with preconceptions. In heaven's name. Then one is as good as another.

I was still thinking about all this long after he and his white-coated followers had left the room.

He'd better not cross my path today. I'd have a fit. Fly into a rage. Get up and smack him. "Your shitty composure makes me puke. Do you really understand what you just said? 'Some problems might come to light in your grandchildren or great-grandchildren.' How can I ever have a child now? I don't want to put a curse on my offspring, to punish my grandchildren and great-grandchildren who may be born crippled because their grandmother or great-grandmother was stupid enough to study at a university somewhere abroad. Just where a nuclear reactor happened to blow up."

Don't get so upset. Be glad you didn't bring a child into the world. At least you haven't burdened yourself with this guilt.

But at the time. No. I was still naive. Still didn't really comprehend my situation. I yearned for reassurance, for words of consolation. Perhaps it isn't all that bad. Am I imagining a lot of it? Putting myself and those around me under stress for no reason? Persecution mania? Radiation phobia?

Once again I let myself be duped by hope. And yet, I knew that the doctor wanted me to be still. To stay calm. With his matter-of-fact words he lied his way across the abyss. To conceal from himself the fact that there was nothing he could do. Doctors have allowed themselves to become slaves to science. They don't rebel. They patch things up. And then they walk around acting like gods to hide their powerlessness from themselves.

I can't lie in bed any longer. My back hurts. I'm going to get up for a while and walk around. But what if the nurse . . . Oh, no, I'm too weak. Maybe I should lie on my stomach.

I wonder if Ralph knows that I . . . ?

Why am I thinking of Ralph now? Why? Do I want him to visit me? To be shocked? Do I want to prove something to him? "See, it wasn't all in my imagination. But I'm ready to take the next step. I don't need to cling to anyone. Good-bye, farewell."

He would shake his head, would say, "There's still a possibility, even if we can't see it at the moment." That's what he'd say. Exactly that.

I must be daft. It's total nonsense. We've been apart for almost half a year. He wouldn't be interested in me. And why should he be. It doesn't concern him anymore.

He came to see me in the hospital. Two days after the miscarriage. Brought me a bunch of flowers. Good manners. I hadn't expected him. As he walked through the door I looked at the flowers in his hand and smiled. I should have looked at his face right away. His pinched lips, his frowning eyebrows. There was a long silence.

"How are you?"

"Not too bad."

Silence. He took a couple of deep breaths, looked intently at his hands, and said softly—I can still hear the forced note in his voice—"This isn't the time or place to reproach you, but I feel as though you deceived me." A pause. I didn't say anything.

"Why did you keep your pregnancy a secret? Shouldn't I have been consulted? Didn't you tell me that you couldn't get pregnant?"

"Yes."

"And . . ."

"Nothing."

"Is our relationship supposed to be based on lies?"

"No."

"I'm in my third year at the university; getting into the program for university lecturers depends on my grades. I haven't had much time for anything else since I joined the professor's research team . . ."

"You can put your mind at rest," I interrupted him, at first softly, my voice rising gradually, until at the end I was shouting. "I'm not pregnant anymore. No one knows if I'll ever be able to have a child! You should have thought it over before you got involved with me. After all, you knew which university I attended."

I was furious. Also unfair. But if he's going to talk about his research team and not even ask what I was thinking, what I was struggling with day after day, why I so badly wanted to have a child—yes, especially now!

"Stop talking nonsense," he said with deliberate calmness.

That made me even angrier.

"The only thing that matters," he said, "is whether I am going to be asked or just ignored."

I should have shown some understanding. Should have explained why I concealed my fears from him. But I was angry and hurt.

"I want to have a child, and I *will* have one, if not with you, then with someone else!"

That instant, full of anger, I didn't know what I was saying. Was shocked to hear my own words. I wanted to hurt him, to make him furious, to provoke him. To finally jolt him into asking, "What's the matter? What's happening with you?"

Instead he got up and left, without saying another word. I might have known. The door closed, and I yelled after him: "Ralph, Ralph, wait, it's only . . ." But he was already gone. And then I closed my eyes and cried and bit my hand. And then the nurse came in and said, "You're not supposed to get upset."

|

No. I don't want him to find out. I'll have to tell my parents so they won't mention anything to him.

Oh, fiddlesticks. I won't say a thing. It's all the same to me whether anyone finds out or not. I now live in the time afterward. In the "aftertime." It is just an unintended encore imposed on me. I've played out my part, and I don't give a damn about what the actors in the supporting cast think or do once they leave the theater.

The next day my parents came. They probably arranged it that way. Mother had dark circles under her eyes; her hands trembled. She nervously kept opening and closing the clasp of her pocketbook; took out a handkerchief and closed the pocketbook again. Opened it once more and put the unused handkerchief back. Father moved about the room as if in a slow-motion film. He smelled of liquor and spoke very slowly as though he had to ponder every word before pronouncing it. And there were terribly long pauses between his sentences, between his phrases. I could hardly stand to listen to him, but whenever he stopped I hoped he would continue. And when he did talk, my one worry was that he would stop talking.

"My child . . . you have to be brave and have faith . . . in yourself; then everything will be all right. No one can say . . .

how your condition, I mean . . . your miscarriage . . . is connected . . . No one knows the amount of radiation you . . . got . . . at that time. No one . . . can say . . . after the fact. We never did talk about that . . . time. I don't know how much they told you . . . there . . . whether you . . . were careful . . ."

"It's all right, Father," I said. "It's all right. Don't worry about it."

Suddenly I was the one reassuring *him,* and he seemed relieved. Maybe it was the tone of my voice. He leaned back, smiled the knowing smile of an old man who has accepted the fact that there is nothing on this earth he can change anymore.

Mother said nothing while Father was speaking. She had pulled her hair back into a tight knot, and for the first time I saw that the roots were completely gray.

"Why did you send Ralph away?" Mother asked, finally leaving her pocketbook alone.

"I didn't send him away," I said. "He left on his own."

"You've been so secretive, so distant. Why didn't you talk to us? Why didn't you tell us you were pregnant?"

"Oh," I said, "it was only a small, quiet hope. But it's all over now . . . doesn't matter anymore. It doesn't make any sense to talk about what happened. Nothing can be changed, influenced, reversed. It was all wrong and futile."

No one spoke. The blood rose to my head, seemed to collect under the top of my skull. I felt an indescribable pressure that increased with every passing second. I thought it would tear me to pieces if I didn't scream, there and then.

"Why was I such a good student? Why did I take the final exam for university admission? Why did I want to go on for advanced study? Why did I go to the Soviet Union, to Kiev? Why didn't anybody keep me from going there? Why didn't they let us leave once we knew what had happened? Why?"

I wasn't asking my parents. No. I yelled the words at the walls, out the window, to some god or other. I was asking fate or some unknown oracle.

Silence. The nurse came in.

"You mustn't get upset."

"Yes," I said, "it's all right."

My parents sat on either side of my bed. I felt Father's big, heavy hand and Mother's soft, gentle touch on my head.

After this outburst I felt relieved; the pressure inside my head was gone. I closed my eyes, forgot the sickroom and the nurse. For a moment, time stood still.

There was no before and no after. No why. Not anymore. Everything was simple and bright and transparent. I felt no inside, no outside. Everything seemed bathed in a bluish white light. For an instant I felt weightless, calm, and relaxed. Pain and death had lost their sting.

The sensation lasted but a moment. To me it seemed infinitely long. Suddenly I knew that time did not exist in a linear extension on one level only. I opened my eyes; I was lying in my hospital bed, and I was aware of everything that had happened, yet I was no longer depressed by the reality.

At that point I looked at you both and you looked at me, and something was different, in me, in you, and between us. All three of us smiled at the same time, nodding at each other. Then you both got up and slowly, wordlessly, went to the door.

The nurse was standing there, silent, surprised. You turned briefly and then you left, and the nurse gently closed the door.

Actually, that was our final good-bye. You know that, don't you. Father. Mother. Everything that happened after that was something else—ineffable, unnameable. Whenever I think of you, I see you standing there in the hospital room that afternoon: I see a kind man, now aged, and a still beautiful gray-haired woman getting up and slowly walking toward the door.

Even when I did what I wanted to do, was going to do and had to do, even as the music grew fainter, I thought back to this moment with you. I saw the same light, experienced the same weightlessness, and felt both of your hands on my head. From that day forth, I was no longer afraid of death.

I reversed myself one more time. I saw Ralph again and asked him to forgive me. But the rift between us remained. It would have been better had I not seen him again. But it probably had to be, was destined somehow to come to an end. Today I feel no resentment toward him and can scarcely understand my despair on that cold winter afternoon.

We had had coffee with my parents, and afterward the two of us went upstairs to my room. You were standing there with your back to me when I heard myself say, "We're just tormenting each other. Perhaps it would be better if we stop seeing each other."

I didn't mean it to sound as final as it did once the words were out of my mouth. I just wanted to know how you would react, hoping you'd take me in your arms and we would be close again, just as we were in the beginning. You were supposed to stroke my head and say, "Darling, how can you say that?" I wanted to feel close to you again.

In recent days we had been seeing less and less of each other. Your research group was taking up most of your time. There was a residue of distrust between us. Now and then we still slept together, but I no longer felt you. When you caressed me, it was as though a sheet of tissue paper were separating us. Sometimes I saw your hands as they touched my skin, my body. But it was as though I were standing off to one side, as though I were watching a film. I had no feelings for you anymore.

Now you simply turned and said, "Maybe you're right."

Only then, what I had already felt but did not want to accept became clear to me: It was over. It would have been stupid to stay together, senseless. The tide had turned long ago.

"Well then, good-bye," I said.

"Good-bye. We can still be friends."

There followed the usual exchange of polite words. We'd had a nice time, that sort of thing. Meaningless phrases that were supposed to cover up an awkward situation. I've forgotten them.

Perhaps fear had taken hold of you long ago. A fear that, had someone mentioned it, you would have emphatically denied. An undefinable, inexplicable fear. Not fear of an unplanned pregnancy. No. It was the fear that with me you couldn't have any children, even if, later on, you would want to. Or at least not healthy children. Perhaps my fearfulness infected you during those months. But even that doesn't matter now.

I still remember my feeling of superiority. You stayed in the room awhile longer, looked around as though you had forgotten something. Forgive me, but at that moment you seemed to me indescribably ridiculous, so gangly, so helpless, your shoulders slightly stooped, not knowing what to do with your hands.

The door closed. I heard his footsteps on the stairs. And sensed that he knew he would never return. Then everything was quiet. Now he's putting on his coat, I thought. The front door opened, and shut. Standing behind the curtains, I watched him crossing the garden, unlatching the gate, and closing it without even once looking back. It was over.

Funny. When something happens that in fact you've already suspected might happen, you're still surprised. Or angry. Or furious. You're unprepared when it hits you. I had played with this scenario many times. I even thought I had already gone through it. But it had always been just a fantasy, never this irrevocable finality. I picked up an ashtray and threw it on the floor. To hell with him. I flung myself onto the bed, then got up again.

Stop being so silly, I told myself, so theatrical. Nothing helped. I watched myself pacing around the room, lying back down on the bed, getting up, and yet I couldn't laugh at myself. Often we play a role for ourselves and for others, pretending we really mean it. But now it was for real and I was behaving as though I were merely acting out a part that I could slip out of once the play was over. Perhaps some heartaches are so overwhelming that we can only behave in the same trite way people always have.

I went to the bathroom and climbed into the tub. The hot water felt like a caress. Slowly I relaxed, washed my hair, deliberately massaged my scalp with my fingertips. Rinsed my hair for a long time, enjoying the warm spray. Then I carefully dried off every square inch of my skin. Very meticulously. Usually I treated my body quite casually. Now I mattered. I was the center of attention. Not because a man was looking at me, because he felt I was important to him. No, rather because I was looking at myself. Because I took myself seriously, because I thought I looked terrific. Tight jeans, a sheer jersey, matching eye shadow. I told my parents I would be home late.

I

I walked the city streets frantically, my heels clattering on the sidewalk. I was talking to myself in a low voice: words, fragments of words, and curses with each step. At first, I ran as though someone were chasing me; then I walked briskly as though I were heading for a specific place; finally, having calmed down somewhat, I strolled through the city as though this were something I did every day.

I decided to phone Anna, a woman who worked at the plant with me. Had trouble dialing. Started over three times. Didn't want to bother anyone. But she was pleased to get my call, and we made a date to get together that evening.

After that, I felt better. As I walked on, I saw that passersby were looking at me from time to time. I thought: There are a lot of nice young men around. Why hadn't I noticed that before? Why shouldn't I be able to find someone who suited me, who would like being with me, and who would consider me a completely normal woman? Why was I so fixated on Ralph? It was then that I decided I would never again tell anyone which university I had attended.

Anna and I went to a discotheque. We stood where we could see the dance floor and where we could also be seen.

I danced like crazy. Intoxicated by the music, I let it flush out my head, sweep it clear. Flung off were all those burdensome thoughts of Ralph. Slowly I became more relaxed.

Then this blond guy who must have been watching me for

quite a while came over. He was a bit shy, rather pale, but he seemed to like me. He kept coming back, asked me to go over to the bar with him. Anna had also found someone. As we repaired our eye shadow in front of the mirror in the rest room, we agreed to go home separately.

I enjoyed being with the blond fellow. It was wonderful to see myself reflected in the eyes of a stranger, to be seen as a healthy, good-looking woman with firm breasts and long, flowing hair. As he watched me move about, I knew he couldn't help thinking of bed. It was all so simple.

That evening I tried out my story for the first time. The emended version of my past. It was easier than I thought it would be. All I had to do was change the name of the place where I had gone to study. Instead of Kiev, I said it was Leipzig. That was a difference of six hundred miles, and all it required was substituting a single word. He asked whether by any chance while I was at the university there I'd met somebody whose name was so-and-so. I didn't know him, but then you can't know everyone.

I felt incredibly good that evening. Enveloped in the illusion that I could change my life story with just one word.

You see, I thought, it does work. What you make of your life is all up to you. You don't have to run after Ralph if he doesn't want you, and if he does, you don't need to be grateful that he'll accept you even with your past, your problems. There are enough men who'd like to be with you. You can take your pick. For instance, this blond fellow who is going to take you home now.

|

I had been out dancing every Friday and Saturday evening since early January, and always someone was interested in me. I was "lucky," and I would take these young men home or go to their places, and they all believed my story.

It was an addiction. At first, I was glad men were even interested in me. Later, I went to the dance hall, looked around, and picked one out.

I felt like a gambler playing for high stakes. Most of the time

I won. They came up to me. I led them on, and then kept them at arm's length, as the situation required. The art of seduction lies in being neither too aggressive nor too off-putting. And fairly soon I had mastered all the nuances.

Rarely was I with the same man for two consecutive weekends. I wanted to keep them from getting to know me better, keep them from getting closer. They must not become aware of my anxieties, the deep, hidden fear that dominated me, and from which I wanted to flee.

I lived only for the weekends. I needed "success" like an addict. Dancing was my medicine, my high, my ecstasy. I danced with my eyes closed, surrendering to the music and rejoicing in the suppleness and agility of my body.

When the dance was over, I didn't want to be by myself and so I always left with a man, one I had chosen. It wasn't hard to bridge this contradiction: to be close to someone, yet at the same time hide myself from him. Knowing it was only for one night, at most two, I could get involved, could give myself. I wasn't afraid to surrender, to lose myself, to be vulnerable. Rather, it amused me to see how these men, in many and various ways, all believed they could know a woman or possess her just because they had slept with her once. They're so conceited. Domineering and at the same time needing to lean on someone. I escaped from them.

Only in the mornings, with my eyes still closed, I sometimes found it unpleasant to smell the odor of a stranger, of an unfamiliar apartment; when the cold morning light came through the window and someone—rumpled and tousled—was lying next to me. Then I would quietly get up, put on my clothes, write a brief note, and disappear. With time I became quite adept at it. Not one of them ever woke up.

Only occasionally did I take any of them home with me. What was I to do with them the next morning? The only thing I liked about that was waking up in my own bed. But sometimes they made a fuss when, under some pretext or other, I would send them away in the early morning.

One thing I knew: No matter what I did, I must never tell them anything about myself. About what made me do what I did. Whether I could ever have children, and, if so, what kind of children they might be. Under what sort of curse they would perhaps be born. I couldn't reveal where I had gotten my degree and what might be in my body from having been there. I couldn't talk about my fear that this seductive young woman might perhaps soon become pale, bedridden, bald, and in need of care. That would have violated the rules of the game, and these rules were quite clear: I want something from you; you want something from me. If you give me what I want, I'll give you what you want, right here and now. Don't talk about yesterday or tomorrow. Don't talk about the future or your problems. Obviously, if I started in on any of that, they'd clear out. Who wants to get involved with a problem case? Especially once he knows what it's all about. No one. There are enough others out there. Why burden yourself? Why?

"Don't bother me with your sentimental crap, honey . . . Come on, forget it . . . We'll have a wild time . . . It's all the same to me . . . Tomorrow? The future? . . . What's that? . . . Tomorrow is the end of the world, my dear." I'd heard all these phrases thousands of times in different situations. I didn't want to hear them again. I didn't feel like giving these men the chance to ditch me, to get rid of me. I'd rather be the one to send them packing.

Should I have tried to talk with them? More often? No! Once was enough. Even now I could kick myself for having done that. I betrayed myself. I was stupid.

I saw him two or three weekends in a row. Even though I knew better, I started to talk:

"Listen, what I told you about where I went to college, that's not quite true. Actually it was in Kiev. And since then I've been afraid that I was exposed to something. And I don't know to how much. I had a miscarriage and now I keep tabs on my body, looking for symptoms every day. When I comb my hair and a few strands fall out, I worry, and when I'm tired or have a headache or look pale . . . I'm always afraid it might be the first indication of radiation sickness."

He asked me whether it was contagious. And after that I had to look for a different discotheque because I had no luck at the old one anymore. At least I wasn't stupid enough to bring that subject up again.

Why are you thinking about these forgettable men? Do you have regrets about that time? Are you longing to return to those days? Would you like to go on that way? Start over again? Come on, that's out of the question! No. Forget it. Forget it all. And quickly. Don't let this clergyman haul you over to the other side.

Maybe I'll tell him about it. Shock him. I'll say, "Give me a new past. Then maybe I'll talk to you about the future." No. What good would that do? I don't want to go on. I don't want to talk to him at all anymore. What I did was my way of coping with my problem. Whether others can accept that or not, I don't care.

And Father's drinking problem got worse. That was his way of escaping from reality. Suicide in installments. I observed it from a tremendous distance. He wasn't actually drunk, but he was never quite sober either. I'm sure it pained him to see how I lived my life. Never bringing home the same young man from one weekend to the next or not coming home at all till the next morning, sleeping till noon, and then going off again in the afternoon.

"Do you have a new boyfriend?" he once asked me, after I hadn't brought anyone home for a while.

"No, I don't."

You looked older, Father, more tired, more worn out. I felt

sorry for you, but what was I to do? Whenever we talked, something we did infrequently, you would close your eyes for seconds at a time. And each time I thought you would never open them again, just so you wouldn't have to see things anymore.

Mother's hair turned gray. She had stopped dyeing it. The piano remained silent. That's how things stood when I missed my period again.

Had I been careful? Careless? Was it intentional or not? But to whom am I accountable? It just happened. I didn't bring on this pregnancy intentionally. Nor did I try to prevent it. True enough . . . *Only a recommendation* . . . My desire for a child, a healthy child, was still there. Even after the first miscarriage. But I allowed fate to run its course. Just as when I was fifteen or sixteen and couldn't make up my mind, I would say: If you catch this bus, you'll go to see him; if you miss it, you'll go home. Chance will decide.

If I were to become pregnant, I persuaded myself, then it was destined to be, then everything would be fine. And if not, then so be it.

It was also a kind of morbid defiance. A desire to know what was what. If you have another miscarriage, then the "recommendation" has turned into a final verdict against which there can be no further appeal. Then what you were afraid would happen actually has happened; then you are sick, you are marked, and your fate is sealed. Then you will have to act accordingly. Like so many others, you'll be a nameless victim, but you won't appear in any statistics as a victim. All that went through my mind as I permitted fate to gamble with something best not left to chance. With death. With life.

This constant urge to wash myself. When my period didn't come, I felt unclean all the time. No sooner had I climbed out of the bathtub or turned off the shower and dried myself with a spotless towel than I thought the air had soiled me again. I actually felt as if small invisible particles were gradually being deposited on my skin, clogging my pores. It took a lot of willpower to keep from washing myself all over again.

I forced myself to go upstairs to my room. I would say, "Get dressed now." Or "Go to bed." But then I would stand there, naked and undecided, unable to move. The only thing I could think of was: You've got to wash yourself! You have to be clean! You mustn't get dirty. If you're not clean, you won't give birth to a healthy child.

Sometimes I stood there like that for half an hour, sometimes a whole hour. Then I went downstairs again.

If, by chance, the bathroom was occupied, it was a catastrophe. I reproached myself. Why did I wait so long? Why didn't I come down fifteen minutes earlier? This quarter hour might have been the decisive one.

Even worse were the days when I had to go to work. On the train for a whole hour. I tried not to touch anything, not to hold on anywhere, to position myself in such a way that someone else would open the door when I had to get off. Once inside the plant, I immediately went to the toilet and washed my hands. I avoided shaking hands with anyone, found it disgusting to touch anything, no matter whether it was paper, wood, or textile. I was revolted by everything. I saw germs, bacteria, viruses, harmful particles everywhere, and I wanted to wash them away, rinse them, rub them off me.

There was little I could still eat. Certainly not the glop we were served for lunch in the canteen. I limited myself to packaged foods in cans or sealed bags that I could open myself. Or I ate fruit I had peeled after having washed my hands. This went on for days, weeks.

|

Until that evening, that Friday evening. How long ago was that? A week? Ten days? No. Impossible. That can't be true. It must have been an eternity ago.

These images. I'll never be rid of them. Even in years to come. If there are years to come.

I

I had taken a bath, gone back up to my room. Everything was quite normal. Having put on a white T-shirt and my long, gray skirt, I was standing in front of the mirror. Without having made any sudden movement, simply out of nowhere, out of the stillness, I felt this dreadful pain, this sharp stabbing pain, and then something warm was running down the insides of my thighs. Horrified I stared into the mirror, not daring to move a muscle; saw myself standing there, petrified. I heard my own crazy laughter, the same laughter I had heard so often in my dreams. It penetrated the entire room, dug its claws into the walls, and the walls spewed it back at me. It sounded dreadfully loud, even though I hadn't made a sound. I could see myself in the mirror, my mouth closed, my face completely immobile. The laughter was going to kill me.

I raised my arms, and put my hands over my ears. And the gruesome laughter actually stopped. Not until some time later did I dare slowly to lower my hands. There was silence. A charged silence, full of tension as though you had tuned in a radio station that was not broadcasting anything at the moment. You don't hear anything, but somehow you know the station is there, silent for the moment, offering no program. Slowly I grasped the neck of my T-shirt with both hands; my fingers clenched, I pulled and pulled, feeling the material strain. It cut into the skin at the back of my neck; finally it gave way and tore open down the front. I kept pulling, inch by inch. The ripping sound broke the tense silence. My breasts were bare. The rip had reached the lower hem of the T-shirt where it again encountered firm resistance. With a yank I tore the last scrap. I put my arms, my shoulders back until my hands were behind my back. Shaking myself lightly, I allowed the torn T-shirt to slide off me. Following an unspoken command, I bent down, grabbed hold of my skirt hem, and with my fingernails I made a small tear and then ripped the skirt evenly upward, section by section. I looked at my feet, my calves, my thighs, and saw the blood running down in small rivulets. I watched, fascinated. When my arms had spread too far apart, I renewed my grip on the material where it divided, and kept tearing. By now I was standing upright again. I looked in the mirror.

There stood a woman whose upper body was naked, whose skirt was torn nearly all the way up. From a spot covered with pubic hair, blood was dripping onto her legs. The blood ran down in fine lines, lines that met and flowed together and then, a little farther on, separated again because of a small hair or a curvature, thus producing an arbitrary pattern. With a sudden wrench, the woman tore the skirt open at the waistband and let it drop to the floor.

She took the middle finger of her right hand and, dipping it in one of the red rivulets on her right thigh, began with gentle motions to distribute the blood. First over her thigh, then carefully moving upward, her finger left reddish brown dots and straight and curved lines on her white skin. Now she used her left hand to take dabs of blood from her left leg and spread it on her belly and breasts. Moving faster and faster, she reached into her crotch to get more of the red liquid which turned dark once she spread it on the surface of her skin. It seemed to become taut as it dried.

I watched with interest what the woman in the mirror was doing. She was a stranger to me. This was not my body, those were not my hands. No, the blood-smeared woman I was watching in the mirror—artfully made up like a film actress—had nothing whatsoever to do with me.

This wasn't a living, sentient body. Of course not. It was a trick. Obviously. After all, I could see how her pointed fingernails were boring into her skin, scratching, digging in deeper and deeper. That must hurt terribly, but I wasn't feeling any pain at all. Therefore I couldn't be this person. It was a hallucination. There was no pain. Merely this gravid pause in an interrupted broadcast, and images. A performance in the mirror: bright red rivulets on the skin of the illusion were mixing with reddish brown paint that was already beginning to dry. But no pain, no pain. It wasn't me. It was only a nightmarish apparition.

I looked at the woman's face. Her mascara was smudged. Black blotches, black lines. She carefully rubbed her fingers along the smudge under one of her eyes. Wanting to wipe away the black, the mourning. Suddenly there was blood on her face. Startled, she stopped and held both palms up to her eyes as though she wanted to read something in them. Infinitely slowly she lowered her eyes.

I looked at my hands as I stood there, motionless, glanced into the mirror, and again at my hands. At last I looked from my mistreated and blood-smeared body to the floor where the torn skirt and the tattered T-shirt lay.

The clock in the room struck the hour. The radio station was broadcasting again. The sound had returned.

This bloody piece of flesh was me. This was my fate. Others had decided it. They had sentenced me, and there would be no appeal. No court would retry my case. The verdict was final.

The clock finished striking and then continued ticking off the minutes of the next hour, softly, serenely.

I

After that it was clear: I would have to live without having children, if I went on living at all. I would live without hair, in hospitals—if you can call that living. The radiation had gotten to me. It made the red flow out between my thighs.

I bent down for my things, crumpled them up, held the T-shirt over my crotch, crept to the bathroom, and locked myself in. A bloody lump dropped out of me and into the toilet. I bit my right hand and flushed the toilet with my left. I flushed and flushed. Flushed away my children and my hopes. In the shower I let the lukewarm water run over my mistreated, burning skin. The water turned red. I stepped out of the shower, patted my wet skin dry, and carefully oiled it. Stuffed my torn clothes into a plastic bag. Took two sanitary napkins, pulled on a pair of panties and a nightgown, went back to my room, and climbed into bed. Feeling I would never wake up again, I fell asleep.

But I did wake up again. Mother came into my room. Drugged with sleep, I said I was tired and didn't want to get up again today, didn't want to eat supper. No, I wasn't sick, just very tired, terribly tired.

Not for a long time had I slept as deeply and soundly as that night.

It was like a miracle. The next morning I was able to get out of bed with scarcely any discomfort. It only felt as though I were having a heavier period than usual. I tried to forget what had happened the previous evening.

I combed my hair, and when the mirror wanted to show me images of the night before I refused to look. I simply closed my eyes. Again I found a lot of hair on my brush, more hair than could ever grow back.

I

What prompted me to go downtown that morning, that Saturday? I no longer know. But in retrospect what happened that day seems logical and obvious.

I took the train past several stops and got off without knowing exactly where I was. Walked a few blocks farther toward a supermarket, even though I had no intention of buying anything. With a gesture of finality, I chucked the plastic bag into a gray garbage dumpster.

A blue baby carriage was standing in front of the store. I walked past it slowly, glad to be rid of my bloodstained things.

A tiny face was peeking out from behind a smoothed coverlet that rose like a mound. A little hat covered most of the baby's hair; just a few stray strands were showing. Two narrow ribbons were tied into a bow under its chin, keeping the hat from slipping off. Plastic balls and cubes were strung on an elastic cord across the front of the carriage—light blue, pink, yellow, and red—two on each side and in the middle, also a little rabbit made of plastic. All out of the child's reach.

The baby lay there quietly with its eyes closed. I took a few hesitant steps, then stopped.

Two gray-brown sparrows were squabbling over a piece of stale bread. The bird that had the bread was being pursued by the other, who attacked him with his sharp, pointed beak. The victim may have had the booty, but he couldn't defend himself. When the pain became too great, he pecked back. That's what the attacker had been waiting for. He snatched the bread the other bird had dropped and tried to get away with it. The pursued became the pursuer; the pursuer, the pursued. They kept exchanging roles, fruitlessly. An elderly woman wearing a sun hat was walking back and forth.

I went into the store, put some things into my basket, baby food, baby juice, milk, and took them to the cash register.

It was so unfair. Here was a woman who had a child. That meant she was healthy. She could have more children. If she wanted to. And, I thought, I have nothing. I'm not well; can't have any children; can only bleed. I'd be a good mother. I didn't do anything wrong. Why me? Why such a fate? Thoughts like that.

My line at the checkout counter moved more quickly than the others. Or did the people in front of me have fewer things in their baskets? I would be a good mother. If that baby carriage . . . It was so absurd. Nearly my turn. If, by the time I got outside, that carriage was still standing there, it would be a sign for me. It would mean I was supposed to take the child. It would be my child. Compensation for the injustice inflicted on me. The baby carriage had been left there for me. Naturally. Suddenly it was all quite clear.

At the cash register I paid and packed up my things. In no particular hurry. It was supposed to be a fair test: If, when I get outside, the carriage is still standing there, then . . . Maybe a woman had abandoned her child? Things like that were possible. Why couldn't I, by sheer coincidence, happen to be at the spot where a woman has abandoned her child? She wants to get rid of the child. Separated from her husband, the child keeps reminding her of him. It's possible.

She wants to get rid of a child, and I want to find one. For once luck might be with me. The baby carriage certainly has been standing out there for an awfully long time. That just isn't normal.

So I went out, deep in thought. The sparrows had disappeared; the woman wearing the sun hat was gone. Only the baby carriage was still there. Again there was no sound; again a silent film was running its course.

|

I put my shopping bag into the net pouch on the baby carriage, released the brake, and pushed the carriage down the street. I pushed it cautiously, neither fast nor slowly; walked away with a clear conscience, felt no fear, no guilt, no thoughts about the child's mother. No. I was the child's mother. This was my child. I had given birth to it. It belonged to me. A pleasantly smiling young man helped me get on the streetcar. His lips moved. He said something like "It's nice to see a happy young mother." There was still no sound. The streetcar started up silently; the houses passed by like pictures, like scenery. I transferred to another streetcar, got off, went for a walk in a park, sat in the sun. Suddenly the two sparrows were back, fighting over the bread. But I didn't have time to watch them. I had to, I wanted to, take a look at my child. It was just opening its eyes, its mouth. It squeezed its eyes shut again, and its face turned red. I thought, It's going to cry; it must be hungry or thirsty. You have to give it something to eat or drink. I rocked the carriage a little and for a second the baby seemed to calm down. Its mouth became small and narrow again. I pushed the carriage along and then I took the train. Arrived home; my parents were standing in the doorway, waiting for me. They waved to me. Mother lifted my child out of the carriage and carried it around in her arms. Joyously she tossed it up into the air. I stood next to her, watching anxiously. I hope she doesn't drop it accidentally. Father took the baby carriage to the shed and came back with a mattress under his arm. The child again opened its mouth. It cried. I flinched. The sound had returned.

The baby really was crying and someone tapped me on the shoulder.

"Are you not feeling well?" a young woman asked me.

Startled, I stared at her. "Oh no," I said, "I'm all right." She was looking at me with kind eyes. If only the earth would swallow me.

"You have a beautiful child," I stammered with great effort, choking down a lump in my throat.

"Is there anything I can do for you?" the woman asked and smiled encouragingly. Her hand touched my arm gently.

"No, no, never mind. It's really very nice of you, but it's all right. Thank you very much and excuse me," I said haltingly, looking down at the ground like a schoolgirl caught doing something wrong. I turned slowly and walked away.

I had gone mad, I thought. Crazy. More and more often now the sound is gone. I get lost in fantasies, torment myself, scratch and mistreat my body without feeling anything. I want to steal other people's children and consider it normal behavior. I even have explanations for what I do. I've gone mad. Fortunately no one has noticed yet. But how long before they do, and what sorts of unpredictable things will I do in the meantime?

I knew what I was doing. It was not a snap decision. No. It had matured over a long period of time. Granted, for others, even those close to me, none of it was easy to see.

The only logical thing to do was to get out of town. Away from people. To be by myself. To make up my mind. That's what I wanted to do. That afternoon. To admit to myself my long-concealed wish.

The train I took went right by our house, and it was as though I no longer lived there, as though I had moved away years ago. I got off at the last stop of the suburban line. Walking down the steps to the waiting room, I pressed my hands against my temples. My head was splitting. The pressure eased somewhat when I got to the nearby woods.

The sun's rays broke through the clouds; the forest was still damp from morning dew or the rain that had fallen the night before. Now steam was rising, and the smell of earth and pine needles and leaves was in the air. In the clearings the ground was already dry. I went farther and farther off the main paths, walked for a while through the tall trees of a timber forest, then past an area of young trees. I stopped before a shimmering spiderweb that had caught some dewdrops which now sparkled in the sun like small crystals. The forest floor exuded a pungent fragrance.

I found a sunny spot and sat down. Gently I ran my hand over the blades of grass that bent under my touch only to spring up again when released. I threw my head back, shook my hair, and gazed at the clouds drifting high above the landscape in a sky so incredibly blue that it looked as though it were always that bright color, as though there never had been a night and as though there would never again be another.

I thought back to my childhood, to trips Mother, Father, and I had taken on our bicycles, carrying on the package racks a basket of apples, sandwiches, and lemonade or a thermos containing hot or iced tea. In those days we, too, would sit on a blanket at the edge of the forest and look up at the sky. We called it a "radiant" sky and did not recoil at the word. We told one another stories. The clouds turned into castles or dragons, princesses, goblins, or monsters; they took the shape of ships with billowing sails that invited us to sail along toward unknown horizons.

Now the clouds were mute. They gathered here and there into dull clumps, only to be torn apart elsewhere by the wind, but they were silent. I ran the fingers of my right hand through my hair. Many strands had been falling out every day. When will it all be gone? How much time do I have? I already knew the answer.

Estimates of damage from the catastrophe were said to be in the billions. Hundreds of billions. I suddenly wanted to know who had made those calculations and how. I would like to know before I die: How much is my life worth? How much is my hair worth? How much for my unborn children? Is there anyone who even knows anything about me? How absurd—converting the priceless, the unmeasurable, into sums of money.

I

But even that afternoon I tried once more to allay my fears. I looked at the hair I had lost and thought: Don't all people lose a few hairs now and then? Maybe I'm imagining all this. A delusion. All psychosomatic. Just a nightmare from which I'll soon awake.

But self-deception didn't work anymore. Fortunately. I thought: Stop fooling yourself! You know better than that. You know the symptoms. The overpowering tiredness that swallows sounds and drives you crazy, that turns clouds into dull heaps, that kills all yearning. The vague feeling of being unwell that has robbed you of joy and enthusiasm and has driven laughter from your life.

Once, I thought, I wanted to do something really important and meaningful. How long ago was that?

Now I spend my time in front of the mirror, counting the hairs on my head, feeling my breasts to see whether I can detect any lumps. I struggle against this vague nausea that comes and goes from one hour to the next and lasts for days. I drag myself along, on the verge of throwing up, afraid to eat because I feel my stomach is filled with fog or smoke that wanders back and forth within me, distending my insides and leaving no room for anything edible. On top of that, the frequent attacks of diarrhea, the fear of dirt, the constant urge to wash my hands even though that didn't save my child. Every day I get thinner and uglier. It's all in vain. It's all muddled, all ruined.

I put my arms on the ground and my head on my arms. For a while I played with the black earth. At some point I fell asleep and dreamed one of my recurring dreams.

I

I am going to a dance wearing a long flowing dress. My black shoes have high heels, but I can walk and dance easily in them. My dancing partner, whom I don't know, has grasped my waist with his right hand; he holds my right hand in his left, far out from our bodies so as to maintain balance. Are we dancing a waltz? I can't hear the music. But all the others seem to hear it. My partner leads me confidently across the dance floor. I fling my head back, letting my hair flow out behind me. I have the feeling that I'm almost floating or flying, everything is so light, I barely feel my own weight. At first other couples are dancing, too; they turn and turn on their own axes, while moving forward along an invisible line describing a large circle. The women are wearing loose filmy dresses, the men dark suits.

I notice one couple moving more and more slowly, finally stopping and walking over to the edge of the dance floor. The other couples do the same. They form a circle and watch us. Alone in the center of the floor, I turn with my partner, who holds me so lightly I hardly notice. We spin rapidly, and the people surrounding us blur into dots of color that whirl in colorful confusion; the music gets faster and faster. I suddenly hear a flourish, and then the music stops.

We stand in the center of the dance floor, our hands disengage, but my partner's right arm still encircles my waist.

We bow, turn once to the right, and again to the right, and again and again. We continue to bow, and when I stand up straight I toss my head far back each time so that my hair flips out in one swinging motion.

After our last bow, the people watching us raise their hands as though to applaud. But suddenly their faces are distorted into grimaces. The women shriek, and the sound turns into the rising and falling wail of a siren. All are pointing their fingers at me. Frightened, I turn around and see my hair sliding like a wig across the parquet floor toward the people who continue to point at me. Horrified, I put both my hands up to my head. I feel my bare skull. There is no skin, just naked bone. I tear myself away from my partner, who tries to hold me back, and I run after my hair; but I don't get anywhere. The floor is terribly slippery. My high heels snap off; I fall but keep sliding on my knees until I'm only an arm's length from my hair. Just then a hand grabs for the shock of hair, picks it up, and passes it around like a trophy. The people laugh and laugh.

I go from one person to the next. I ask, I plead with them to give me back my hair, but I'm always too late; the hair has already been passed on, tossed to the next one, and the person I'm pleading with shrugs his shoulders, "I'm sorry, I can't help you."

I

When I woke up in the clearing I put my hand up to my head. I felt my hair and, relieved, I closed my eyes and took a deep breath. But the growing relief I felt with each breath I took could not banish the ugly dream.

Softly, almost whispering, I said to myself: "Do something. Stop being a victim. You know how to put an end to this nightmare that's become your life. Now, finally, take charge. Don't wait until you succumb, inundated by a flood of voracious, rampantly proliferating cells. Don't just sit there doing nothing, watching with that everlasting passive, wait-and-see attitude, placing the responsibility for your life in the hands of others. You know what you have to do. Deep down you've known for a long time. You've just hidden it from yourself."

I

The separation from Ralph, the desperate obsessive behavior on weekends, the denial of my past, putting my room in order, throwing away letters and notes—these were all logical, sequential steps. And now I had reached my goal, and nothing was left undone; no longing, no hope tied me to this life anymore. I felt an inexplicable, rare harmony with myself. The nightmare was nullified. In spite of myself, I had to smile.

I was free, freer than I had been at any other time in my life. This was why I no longer had to respond to any of those vague powers that had governed my life up to now. Did not have to submit to those nightmares, did not have to kowtow to the general belief that "one has to live," or bow to the ostensible obligations to the so-called progress for the well-being of humanity. No. I no longer needed to take any self-appointed authorities seriously or expose myself to the leering looks of men. No. Even an unpredictable insidious illness could no longer touch me. Once I had decided what I must do, that decision was all that counted, and all other powers and rules became invalid, unimportant.

It was an overwhelming realization: I myself can decide. I can command when the sun will stop in its path. One simple order from me: "Stand still, sun!" and it would stand still forever. Or that evanescent cloud up there, above the tip of the tall pine tree; it would pause and never move on. At the factory, trousers and jackets would continue to be manufactured for warehouses, without me. I no longer had to search, to try so hard, to hope, and to deceive myself. I no longer had to envy others who had been spared, spared so far. On the contrary, suddenly they seemed pitiful to me. They still had ahead of them what already lay behind me. They were still running around in circles, forced to do things they didn't want to do, persuaded or pressured by apparent necessities, by ideologies, by their own desires. They did not know their own strength, didn't realize that they themselves had put on the shackles that would later destroy them, did not see that they could choose, at any time. Something kept this insight from them, just as it had kept it from me until now.

I also thought of my parents. Of the scene in the hospital after my miscarriage, of our silent agreement. But I did not want to and could not keep going, to see how things would turn out, just for their sake. No. One day they would understand. I hoped.

What choice did they have? Either to nurse a daughter, ill with radiation sickness, until she died, to live with her gradual decline, or to say to themselves, sooner or later: Yes, our daughter has left us. She herself made that decision.

Eventually, every daughter leaves her parents' home. Except I would no longer be within reach. Never again. That's true. But at least they would be able to remember me the way I am now, I thought. Perhaps Father would stop drinking; perhaps Mother might one day sit down at the piano again, in spite of everything, and play, and remember our playing together; then music would float through the house. I don't want my parents ever to see me bald, emaciated, withered.

It was absurd.

In this unbearable situation, just when I was ready to die, I suddenly won back the freedom to live.

During those few minutes I was happy again. Suddenly I could smile, even laugh, entirely unforced and without inhibition. Everything around me became light and cheerful, the birds, even the bugs; the clouds seemed to share my joy. The painful separation between me and the world had vanished. I was at one with it. Even after I am gone, I felt, I would remain here in some indefinable way.

But I knew very well that this transformation would be brief, a few hours at best, made possible only by the imminent end. If this beautiful moment of indescribable lightness and happiness were to weaken my readiness to die, even for a few seconds, then everything I had just shaken off would again take hold of me. The "recommendations" and verdicts, the fears, the unbearable uncertainty. I would constantly be grasping at a life that was eluding me, and in this futility I would once again waste my days, conform, and permit myself to be pressured.

Only a few things were still undone. I would have liked to say something to my parents to console them. Most of all I wanted to let them in on my plans. But the way things are, you have to steal away like a thief in the night. And pity you if you're not quick enough; you'll be violently yanked back. Back to a hospital, attached to an IV drip, and you're again in the place you'd said good-bye to once and forever.

It wasn't a snap decision. No, my decision had ripened over a long time. It was a step into freedom. True, an absurd form of freedom. One step into the void that beckons, offering incredible harmony and infinite peace.

And one other thing was clear to me: Earlier in my life, if I had occasionally thought about the fact that I would have to die one day, I wouldn't have taken so seriously many of the things that came along, blown out of all proportion. I wouldn't have let myself be so easily deterred, placated, intimidated. Perhaps I would have escaped from Kiev. Back then. Without permission. Would have thought up some pretense. Would have dispensed with the exams.

I wouldn't have kept quiet about the things that happened there, would have talked to that writer about my dreams, my fears, would have described what they did with us, what we let them do to us. I wouldn't have been so naive as to believe that I could be spared as long as I behaved well and kept quiet, and tried to forget.

Everything would have appeared in a different light. Because behind all the fear I so often felt and that caused me to hold still, to conform, to keep quiet, there was always the fear of death, a death you can't elude anyway. Had I thought about death, I would have looked things more clearly in the eye, and not allowed myself to be lulled and lied to so much.

That afternoon I went home and my decision was firm. The clouds were telling stories again; I thought of a song:

> Bless you, leaves, bless you, grass,
> Bless you, everything that ever was,
> For now I have to die.

But I didn't have to; I had decided to. I wanted to die at that hour. And it was easy for me.

When I arrived home I embraced my father, kissed him on the cheek. I patted my mother's hand and said she ought to play the piano again, that I would like that very, very much. Then I quietly took my leave from them and hoped they would be able to forgive me.

|

I sat in the garden, breathed in the fantastic spring fragrance, collected the colors with my eyes, and when I didn't find a particular color right away, I looked for it in the flowerbeds or in the grass. I wanted to take them with me, just as I wanted to take the songs of the birds with me. I wasn't tired. I felt well. I was hungry: I drank some coffee. I ate some cake. And the sun seemed more bearable than usual . . .